PLAY ROOM

A Society X Novel

HEIDI MCLAUGHLIN
L.P. DOVER

play room

New York Times and USA Today Bestselling Authors

HEIDI MCLAUGHLIN
L.P. DOVER

Play Room: A Society X Novel
L.P. Dover & Heidi McLaughlin
Copyright 2017 by L.P. Dover & Heidi McLaughlin
Editor: There for You Editing Services
Cover Design by: Letitia Hasser at RBA Designs

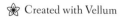 Created with Vellum

For all the fans, readers, and those who get lost in
Society X

ONE

Kai

---

*P*arker Ward stands at the podium, poised and ready to start his annual meeting. For the past six months, he has been asking me to come work for Ward Enterprises to start his community redevelopment division. It wasn't until he offered me a shiny penthouse overlooking the city of Portland that I finally agreed.

As I cast my gaze around the conference room, I notice everyone has their attention on Mr. Ward. He speaks eloquently about the services his company provides the surrounding areas. That is why I'm here. He brought me in to revitalize a failing community. It's my job to bring life back into it, which is easier said than done. Although with the financial backing of Ward Enterprises, anything can be easy.

"Over the years, Ward Enterprises has expanded business into many different aspects. Recently, instead of buying out a sinking fashion company, we partnered and launched our own fashion line. It is with that success that we were approached to give back to the community. It's easy to make a donation and watch others do the work, but

Ward Enterprises is above that. When we do something, we do it at one hundred percent, which is why I created the Community Redevelopment Project.

"CRP will help rehabilitate neighborhoods that come to us for help. Their spokesperson must show us where they have tried and failed to raise the funds needed. The board will listen, assess, and review the application and oral presentation. We will also go to the city and see. We will watch the community interact, and see if they're a viable investment for Ward Enterprises. There will be some that we have to say no to, but that doesn't exclude them from applying later."

The man beside me leans over. "You new here?" he asks, interrupting Parker's speech. He extends his hand and we shake. "I'm Bryant Frazier. I work in Marketing."

"It's nice to meet you, I'm Kai—"

"And now I'd like to introduce you to Kai Robicheau, the new director of the Community Redevelopment Project. Kai's first major project will be Sweet Briar," Parker explains. Everyone starts clapping as I stand and reach for the button on my suit jacket. I grin at the man next to me and make my way to the podium where I shake Parker's hand.

"Thank you for the warm welcome," I say into the microphone. "I am very happy to be here and get started on bringing life back to Sweet Briar. Today, I will make my first official trip out there. Over the past few months, Mr. Ward and I have gone out and met with Pastor Larry and gone over what the community needs. Our first plan will be to build some low-income housing and reopen the strip mall that's there. It'll be our focus to bring industry back to Sweet Briar and generate a tax base. If anyone would like to tag along, please let me know." A few people laugh, but only Bryant raises his hand. I nod toward him. "Thank you!"

After making my way back to the table, Bryant shakes my hand again. "Mr. Ward has been talking about you, says we're to give you whatever you want."

"Really? No budget?"

He shakes his head. "Sweet Briar has a special place in his heart. It's where his grandmother was born and raised."

It all makes sense now why Sweet Briar is the first official town for this project. I would do the same thing if my grandparents needed help.

Parker speaks for a few more minutes before he excuses everyone. I'm barely out of my seat before others are coming over to introduce themselves. I find out quickly that my assistant's name is Brittany, and she's here to make sure my job is easy. I can already tell that I like her, although I have a strict 'no fraternizing with co-workers' policy. I did that once and it turned out bad. So bad, in fact, that I quit my job and moved away.

"Are you serious about heading out to Sweet Briar with me?" I ask Bryant.

"Of course," he replies.

I motion for him to follow me out of the conference room, only to have Parker call my name.

"I see that you've met Bryant," Parker says, nodding toward the man.

"Yes, he's going to head out with me. I'm going to meet with Pastor Larry and let him know that we'll to get started on Monday."

"Perfect. If you need anything, let me know." Parker pats my shoulder before disappearing down the hall.

"So tell me what it's like to work at Ward Enterprises?"

3

I ask Bryant as we ride the elevator down to the parking garage.

He shrugs, but I can tell he's happy. "Hard and rewarding. Ward doesn't mess around. He's a shark, but treats all of his employees well."

"That's good to hear." I point at my car and climb into the driver's seat. The GPS already has Sweet Briar plugged in and ready to go when I start my car.

"Nice ride." He strokes the dashboard of my Z4 Roadster.

"Came in handy when I was living in Malibu," I tell him as we pull out of the parking garage. Of course, it's raining, which means I won't be able to put the top down. That was the luxury I gave up in order to move here—sun and warmth all the time—but I believe in this project and Ward's vision.

It's almost an hour before we arrive in Sweet Briar, which is out toward the coast. I can already tell that I'm going to have to be strategic when I'm going to be working on site or the office. Traffic is heavy, but nothing compared to what we'd experience in Los Angeles.

When we arrive, I show Bryant where we are breaking ground on Monday for the housing project. I also reveal what the apartments will look like. We're installing a playground to give the children a place to play, along with a swimming pool. Next, I take him over to the rundown strip mall that I will be working to bring business back to, starting with a grocery store.

"This is a huge project," he says as we survey the grass-riddled parking lot of the shopping center.

"I know." The toe of my shoe kicks up a clump of grass.

"No pressure, right?" he laughs as I shake my head.

He has no idea. I left a very cushiony job in Malibu

doing urban development to take this job. Failing isn't an option for me. There is too much at stake, even more knowing that this town has more meaning to Parker than another destitute location.

Bryant rattles off his ideas for the shopping center, and even though this isn't his specialty, he has a lot of great ideas. Many are things I might implement in the development plan.

Bryant cocks his head to the side, stroking his chin. "This will be good."

"I agree. Ward Enterprises is doing a good thing by helping out the struggling community."

We head inside the buildings and I show Bryant a few of the plans. The stores will be rebuilt to suit the needs of the retailer. No more of this one size fits all type construction. Those types of buildings don't work for smaller vendors.

"What do you say we go grab a late lunch," Bryant suggests.

"Yeah, I could go for some grub. Why don't you show me your favorite place?"

"I know just the spot," he replies, laughing.

Getting back into the car, we head toward downtown. Bryant gives me turn-by-turn directions until he has me pulling into a somewhat empty parking lot. The restaurant doesn't have windows, and I have feeling that we're about to have lunch at some mediaeval reenactment dungeon where the waitresses are dressed like wenches and the entertainment like Josephine Bonaparte.

"What is this place?" I ask, making sure my car is locked.

Bryant chuckles and pats my back, leading me toward the building. He holds the door open and once I step in, a small sense of fear and curiosity starts to take over my senses. The hallway is dark with a faint sound of music. "Um ..."

"Trust me." He pushes me forward until we get to the end of the hall where a large window is. Bryant shows the lady something and she smiles.

"Fill this out," she says, sliding a small sheet of paper forward. It asks for my name, address, and phone number.

Glancing from her to Bryant and back at the sheet, I shake my head.

"Trust me," he says again. "You'll enjoy lunch."

I shrug, write down my info, and hand it back to her. Almost immediately, a door opens and a big, burly man beckons us in. "Stay here," he tells us. Honestly, I don't know where he thinks we'll go. The space we're in is dark, louder than it was in the other room.

"Hello, Bryant. Who's your friend?" A young woman appears, as if out of thin air. She's tall with short, jet-black hair and dressed in a black and white ensemble. In fact, the man behind us is in a tux.

"This is Kai Robicheau. He's new in town, and I thought what a better way than to introduce him to Society X." Bryant grins at me.

"I'm sorry, where are we?"

"I'm Jenica, welcome to Society X." Taking me by the hand, she leads me through another a curtain and along a wall, into a space that has my mouth dropping open. Inside the wide-open room, front and center, is a stage with a woman stripping. All around the room, men and women are watching her. Along the back wall, the bar is full with half the patrons being served by scantily clad women.

Running my hand through my hair, I'm at a loss for

words. Bryant has a shit-eating grin on his face and he's laughing. "I know what you're thinking."

I snort. "Actually, I don't think you are."

Jenica leads us to a table and tells us that someone will be over to take our order. I sit, but with extreme caution, not knowing when the last time the leather seat has been cleaned. "I thought you meant food," I tell him as I look around. "Lunch usually equates things to eat."

He laughs again before angling his seat toward the stage. "Sometimes a little liquid is the best lunch."

I stare at him like he'd lost his fucking mind. "And Ward is okay with this?"

Bryant shrugs, and I know right away that the only thing I'll drink today is water. Getting drunk at lunchtime isn't something I pride myself on.

"What is this place?" I ask, glancing around the room.

"We're an exclusive club, Mr. Robicheau," Jenica answers, returning in time for my question. "Let me give you a tour." She takes my hand, whether I had any intention of going with her or not. I think about looking back at Bryant, but have a feeling his eyes are focused on the new dancer who just came onto stage.

Jenica takes me down a hall, stopping at a door where she puts a code into a keypad. "Welcome to Society X, Mr. Robicheau. We are Portland's only exclusive sex club that offers its clients the utmost anonymity. What happens here ... stays here."

"I'm sorry, what?" Eyes wide, I stare at her in disbelief.

She goes to another door and opens it. Inside, there's a large, semi-circular couch, centered in front of a stage. On said stage is a couple, going at it as if this was their last time together.

"Should we be in here?" I blink a few times, thinking I

had to be seeing things. When I open them, the couple is still going at it, the sound of their bodies slapping together. What the fuck have I entered?

"Yes, they like to be viewed. This is the viewing room. Follow me."

It takes me a few seconds to peel my eyes away. I'm a red-blooded male and would be a fool to pass up real-life porn. The next room she calls the dark room, and explains that this is the place everyone should use once because it's the best way to get to know your partner.

"Our third room is the play room." She opens the door and it's bare.

"What goes on in here?" It doesn't even compare to the others.

"Whatever you want. If you're into spankings, role playing, candle play, it can happen in here."

I shake my head. "I'm sorry, but this isn't me."

"That's what they all say." She hands me a document titled Society X Application. "Read it and fill it out before you leave." Tossing me a wink, she leaves me in the room. There is no way I would ever do anything like this, but I have a feeling that if I don't hand this back to her, she'll lock me in some hidden room. Who knows, I'd probably like it, but this place isn't for me. I have a reputation to protect.

Without reading fully, I fill out the questions, writing down the most ridiculous answers I can think of. I have nothing to lose since I will never set foot in this building again.

TWO

Alexandria

"*Who* made the exquisite quiches? They're so good. I think I've had seven of them already." I recognize the voice. It's Evelyn Chambers, a sweet old lady I've known ever since I was a little girl. She lives in Sweet Briar, just like most of the other ladies in the group. I left the small town over a year ago, but everyone still remembers me.

I can't help but smile as I refill the empty platters with more miniature spinach and swiss quiches. I'm too modest to say it was me who made them, even though most of the women know it's me. My boss, Sandy Bruner, my parent's neighbor and dear friend, walks over to the table and points at me.

"Who do you think made them? Alex is the best chef I have on my team."

She waves me over and I join her, greeting the old ladies with a smile. I see them every Saturday afternoon for brunch. It's actually pretty interesting hearing the kinds of things old ladies talk about. Never in a million years did I imagine I'd hear stories of their sex lives. One of the ladies lost her husband while having sex. He keeled over right after coming.

"Good afternoon, ladies. It's good to see you again."

Evelyn with her short, white hair and thick, purple glasses shoves another quiche in her mouth. "These are incredible. Is there any way to get the recipe?"

Giggling, I place my hands on my hips. "Now, now, Evelyn. You know I can't give you that. It's my secret recipe."

She purses her lips and sulks like she always does. "Fine, but I want to take the leftovers home."

Sandy winks at me and tries to hold back her laugh. Evelyn does the same thing every Saturday, requesting my recipes and threatening to keep all the leftovers. Sandy doesn't mind since Evelyn pays for it all and the parties are always at her house. Since her husband died, meeting with her other widowed friends for Saturday brunch is what makes her happy.

Once the party's over, two of my other co-workers and I help Sandy load the empty trays into the catering van. Let's Get Baked Catering Services has been around since before I was born. I even worked at the café Sandy owned when I was in high school. Unfortunately, it had to close due to the slow market. That's why now she just has the catering company and moved it to Portland since it was a bigger city than Sweet Briar. I'm the only employee who's stayed with her through thick and thin. The money isn't the best in the world, but Sandy needs me. My dream is to have my own catering company one day, but it takes money to do that.

"I think that's it, ladies. I hope you have a wonderful weekend."

"You too," Adrienne says, giving her a quick hug.

Dani hugs her as well. "Thanks, Sandy. We'll see you on Monday."

Sandy hugs me and I squeeze her tight. "Take care. I'll come up with some new recipes for next Saturday."

"I'm counting on it," she replies with a laugh.

Getting in her van, she waves at us and pulls out of the parking lot. Dani and Adrienne are waiting by my little silver Toyota Camry. They've grown to be not only my co-workers but friends as well. They're different from my other group of friends, more exciting and full of life.

"Nice job on the quiches," Adrienne calls out. "I think you're going to have to make me some to take home."

I shrug. "As long as you make me your famous chocolate chip cookies."

She holds out her hand. "Deal."

After shaking her hand, I lean against my car. "What are you ladies doing tonight?"

Dani checks her reflection in my sideview mirror and fluffs her hair. "I have a date. Hopefully, it goes well."

I went to high school with Dani, but she graduated two years ahead of me. She has shoulder-length, curly brown hair with thick thighs and a curvy backside. Her husband cheated on her last year and she's made it her goal to lose the weight even though I think she looks great. She's surrounded by more men than I could ever dream of. Sometimes I wish I had her problem. My only issue is that I'm clueless when it comes to men.

Adrienne waves her off. "You'll be fine. Just don't have sex with him." Adrienne's around thirty-five, and ten years older than me, with an amazing body and gorgeous blonde hair. She's also happily married with a kid on the way.

Dani scoffs. "Please, I have no intention of sleeping

with him." Then she winks at me. "At least, not until the next date."

"How do you find the confidence?" I ask her.

Her smile fades. "What do you mean?"

I can feel the heat rise to my cheeks. "You're comfortable with your body and with men. I don't know how to be like that."

Dani and Adrienne glance at each other and they snicker. "Alex, please tell me you're not still a virgin," Adrienne says, completely shocked.

It's embarrassing to admit, but I am. "Is that bad?"

Dani puts her arm around me. "Not at all. It's just rare to find a woman your age who hasn't had sex. However, I do remember you being somewhat of a goodie goodie in high school."

She's right. I was, and everyone from my past still sees me as Alexandria Miller, the girl who never does anything wrong. "Why do you think I moved away? If it wasn't for Sandy, I wouldn't be here."

Most of the guys I've tried to date can tell I'm a virgin the first timethir they kiss me. It's the reason they all run away. I'm inexperienced and they don't want a woman who doesn't know what she's doing. My parents were really strict growing up, so dating was out of the question. It took going to college to find a semblance of freedom. It's a freedom I haven't been able to let go of. I love being on my own, except it does get kind of lonely. That's why I concentrate on cooking and figuring out new recipes.

"Do you want me to see if my husband has anyone he can set you up with?" Adrienne asks.

I shake my head. "It's no use. I don't know how to be intimate with men."

Dani snorts. "It's not hard, sweetheart. You're gorgeous

with that sexy brown hair with blonde highlights, glittering green eyes, and luscious lips. Any man would be lucky to have you. When you like a guy, you get to know them and then you do whatever your body tells you to. Easy peasy."

"Easy for you to say, you have experience. The closest I've come to sex is kissing. I know what happens during sex, it's just the getting to that part I need help with."

Adrienne steps closer and lowers her voice. "Have you ever tried watching porno?"

My cheeks flame bright red, but not out of guilt. I shake my head. "I was always afraid of getting a virus on my computer. Don't get me wrong, I've been curious, but I was always too afraid to click the links."

She waves me off. "You'll be fine. If you want to know about foreplay, just watch some videos on it. Trust me, the things a man can do for you are insane. My husband and I have a pretty healthy sex life."

"Obviously." Laughing, I glance down at her belly.

"You could always try out that club in downtown Portland," Dani suggests. "My cousin goes there and she loves it. She has sex with random guys in the dark room. It's her favorite."

"Wait, what?" I shriek. "What club is this?"

After fumbling around in her purse for a few moments, Dani hands me a business card. "It's called Society X. Basically, it's a strip club with other benefits. She's tried to get me to go, but I haven't had the courage to try it out yet. It's supposedly a whole different world there." She winks. "But if you become a member like my sister, you get to reap the rewards of the sex rooms. Like I said, the dark room's her favorite. It's pitch black and she goes in there with another man she can't see. They can do whatever they want. There's also a viewing room, but she doesn't like that one. I think next week she's going to try the play room."

Adrienne blows out a sigh. "Holy shit, that sounds intense. If I wasn't happily married I'd have to try it out."

"What's the play room?" I ask, completely intrigued. I thought clubs like that only existed in the movies. Who would've thought there'd be one in real life?

Dani's eyes twinkle. "It's a room for anything basically. If you don't want sex, you can find a partner who just wants oral. Or if you have a foot fetish, you can be paired with someone who wants to suck your toes. Whatever you want, you can get. The people you get paired with aren't allowed to know your name or anything about you. It's all anonymous."

My whole body tingles with the idea of being able to go in there without any judgements and be able to live out the inner fantasies I've kept hidden for so long. It seems surreal, but then reality hits me like a ton of bricks. Shaking my head, I hand Dani the card back.

"Sorry, D. It's just not for me."

I say it, but I know the truth. I'm going to check out Society X.

THREE

Kai

_____

*M*y arms quiver as I lower myself to the ground. My chest barely touches the mat before I push myself back up and grunt out, "Twenty-five." Pulling my knees up, I lean all the way back so I can stretch my muscles out before starting another rep of push-ups.

The gym is bustling with people, mostly women with a majority of them using the treadmills. Up until this week I've never had a problem working out, but I find it hard to concentrate with all these hot, sexy chicks flaunting their curves in their skintight spandex pants. Never have I had this problem or felt like I'm chomping at the bit to get laid until my haphazard lunch with Bryant when the only thing served was a plate of tits and a buffet of pussy.

It's some kind of fucked up sorcery—that place he took me to. I can't get it out of my mind, and I have never been one to visit titty bars or gentlemen clubs.

I've done all of my dating through friends, or there's been a time or two when I've gotten online and chatted with a few women. Mostly those turned out to be straight up hook-ups. You spend so much time sexting that while you're trying to make it through the meal all you can do is think about the nudes the lady across from you has sent and count the minutes until you're at each other's place.

Starting the next rep, I lower myself to the ground, exhaling on my way down. The intake of air is supposed to help me rise up, but the strain is real. This is my forth set, and while I'm not out of shape, my body is burning. I pound out as many as I can, choosing to rest in a two-minute plank before making my way over to the treadmill.

As my luck would have it, the only one available is between two hot chicks—one blonde and one brunette. Both with asses that make my mouth water. I really need to get laid.

"Hey, good looking," another hot chick says as she walks by. As if by instinct I turn, only to watch her walk up to another guy. He's fucking huge and looks like he could break me in half. Instead of heading to the treadmill, I turn toward the locker room.

Cutting my workout short is never favorable. In fact, it makes me feel like a failure. I pride myself on staying in shape, following a healthy diet, even when I'm on the road. I am the type of guy who sends his suits out for dry cleaning, who likes his shoes polished, but I can also be laidback. Give me the sun and some bitchin' waves and I'll surf the shit out of them.

Now that I have extra time, I decide to head home to take a shower. So far, I like Portland, at least what I have seen. I thought about asking Bryant to show me around, but fear I might end up tied to a bed at a brothel or bent over some slab of wood, getting my ass whacked by a leather whip. Bryant may be into that freaky shit, but I certainly am not.

Jogging back to my apartment, I opt to take the stairs

over waiting for the elevator. All I can think about is how long it's been since I've had sex. Never, in my life, have I been like this. Usually a quick hand job and I'm good to go, but Rosie and her sisters aren't getting the job done, apparently.

Stripping out of my gym clothes, I step right into the shower, not minding that the water is freezing. I give myself a minute before I look and find my dick bobbing against my stomach.

"Mother fucker," I mutter as I grip him hard. It feels good, but it's not enough. With my other hand braced against the wall, I imagine all the women I saw today, without clothes and ... spinning around a stripper pole.

"You've got to be fucking kidding me," I say, pumping hard. Since when do I find that attractive? I never have, so why now? I reach for my shampoo and dump a handful over my clenched hand for lubrication. In my mind, I'm tricking my dick into think he's being lubed up by something else.

"I need to get laid." My breathing turns labored as my hand slides over my shaft. My hips start to buck, my feet slip, and my free hand is now grasping the showerhead so I don't crash into the wall or fall on my face.

That would be an epic story to tell in the office. *"Hey, new guy, what happened to your face?"*

"Oh nothing, just a little hand job gone crazy this morning."

My inner musings are prolonging the situation. I imagine any girl that I know, bent over the side of my couch with my hands gripping her hips while I pound into her sweet pussy.

"Ahh," I groan as my release comes hot and fast. "Finally."

I wash my hands fully before proceeding to take a shower.

The last thing I need to do is show up at work looking like what's his face from *Something About Mary*. As funny as that movie is, I have a feeling that if Mr. Ward asked me what's going on and why I had sperm gel in my hair, I don't think he'd appreciate my answer of, "You see, boss, Bryant took me to a strip club and now I can't get it out of my head." I'd be fired on the spot, and that isn't something I want to happen.

Dressing quickly, I decide to let my hair air dry. The drive to Ward Enterprises is rather short, but due to the high volume of downtown traffic it takes me longer than necessary.

Thankfully, when I step into the elevator, it's all men, which helps with my earlier problem. If I can avoid being near women for a bit, I'll survive the day. As much as I don't want to, I'm going to have to seek out some one-night stands. Which means finding the city's hotspot and wooing some women.

It has to be one night because I am in no way capable of a relationship right now. The hours that I keep do not bode well for new relationships, and that would be unfair to whomever I wanted to date. I figure with a place as big as Portland, I'm bound to find a few women who won't mind some no strings attached sex.

Stepping into my office, there's a vase of fresh flowers on the small circular table in my office. I'm assuming Ward's assistant put them there. I've never been much of a flower guy, which is probably why my last girlfriend broke up with me.

The chair at my desk is leather, and soft against my fingertips. Ward promised me the world if I took this job and so far he's kept his word. I pull out the chair and sit down, sinking into the luxuriously fine material.

"I see you're settling in," Ward's voice echoes through my office.

Sitting up straight, I motion for him to come in ... not that he needs an invitation. "Just admiring the chair, sir."

"Please, call me Parker," he says, sitting down across from me. "Tell me about Sweet Briar."

Leaning forward, I rest my clasped hands on the top of my desk. "Sweet Briar is one of those places that time forgot."

"What do you mean?" he asks, interrupting me.

"The city built up around it and people left the small town for the bright lights. Towns like Sweet Briar were swallowed up. One problem with every city is weak infrastructure, over usage of cars and roads that aren't wide enough to accommodate the traffic. People opt to live in the city or close to work, instead of living in the small communities."

"And we change that?"

I shake my head. "We can't do anything about the roads, but we can bring the town back to life. With the brand new grocery store and strip mall, it'll appeal to buyers. Particularly families who are looking to escape the hustle of the city for the quiet life."

Parker seems to like what I'm saying, which I suppose if he didn't I wouldn't be here. Thing is, I'm good at my job. He knows this.

"Sweet Briar holds a special place in my heart. I'd like to see it become a thriving community again."

"Me too, sir ... I mean Parker."

"You'll get used to it," he tells me, but I'm not so sure. There's an air about Parker that demands respect. "How's everything else? Portland treating you well?"

As well as a city full of temptation can. "It's great. I have an amazing view of Mt. Hood from my apartment."

"Do you ski?"

I shake my head. "Not unless skiing is code word for surfing."

Parker laughs. "I'm with you there. I'm not a big fan of the winter either. But the mountain is beautiful if you do find yourself up that way. Let me know if you need anything," he says, standing. "You'll find everyone very accommodating here. And keep me updated on Sweet Briar. I'm interested in the progress."

"Will do," I tell him just as he leaves. I half expected Parker to hover over me to make sure I'm doing the job to his specifications. I honestly wouldn't be surprised if he showed up there from time to time. It just means that every day, I need to be on the top of my game.

FOUR

Alexandria

_____

*F*lipping through the channels does nothing to curb my curiosity. Why did Dani have to show me that card? I'm not the type of girl who goes to clubs, let alone sex ones. Deep down, it sort of feels like a lie. Like I've been lying to myself. Maybe I am the kind of girl who likes those things. I've never given myself a chance to explore my hidden desires.

I turn off the TV and grab my laptop, typing in the words *Society X* in the search engine. The website pops up and I click on it. There are pictures of the inside with all the expensive furnishings. It looks very professional and not cheap or dirty at all. The reviews are even top notch and written by multiple celebrities.

Heart racing, I close my eyes. "Am I seriously going to do this?" I glance at the screen again and sigh. "I guess I am." It's only seven o'clock. If I don't like it, I can leave and get back at a decent time.

Hurrying to my room, I rummage through my clothes and settle on a silver sequin top, black pants, and my silver heels. It doesn't take long to get to the club, and when I pull into the parking lot, there's already a line wrapped around the building. I shiver as I get out of the car. Whether it's from the cold breeze or my nerves, I don't know. Taking a deep breath, I make my way to the end of the line. There's a group of girls standing together who all look around my age. I hope like hell none of them know who I am. The last thing I want is for my family to find out what I'm doing.

More people get in line behind me and I feel safe hidden between all the people. No one seems to care that I'm by myself. Luckily, the line moves fast.

"ID, please," the bouncer asks, holding out his hand. He says it very professionally, which catches me off guard. In the movies, when you see club bouncers they're always huge and rough looking. Not this guy. He's still big and muscular, but dressed in a crisp, black tux. I show him my ID and he nods for me to go inside.

Once inside, I'm ushered to a desk where everyone in front of me hands over their belongings to a woman behind the counter. She looks to be in her mid-twenties with black hair and light brown eyes, dressed in a female version of a tux. Judging by the rest of the employees, they all have on the same thing. There's a sign that says no phones, cameras, or electronic devices allowed inside the club. When it's my turn, the woman smiles at me and I hand her my purse.

"Is this your first time?" she asks curiously, raking her gaze down my body.

I nod. "Is it that obvious?"

Biting her lip, she looks down at my body again. I've never had a woman check me out before. "Kind of. You seem nervous."

I am, but I don't want anyone to know that. Casually, I shrug. "I'm fine. Just ready to see what it's all about."

She nods toward the main door where another perfectly coifed man in a tux stood. "He'll lead you in the right direction."

The last of the group before me walks past the other guy, and when I stop in front of him, he smiles. "There are two rooms down the hall. If you want to watch men on stage, go through the one that's labeled *men* and vice versa if you prefer women."

"Thanks," I say, hurrying past him.

I glance down both hallways and head toward the men's side. The music thumps behind the door and I know I have to open it before a line forms behind me. Taking a deep breath, I open it. Women are everywhere around the stage, hollering at the guy onstage who's dancing around with a hard-on. Frozen in place, I can't pull my eyes away from the stage. There are people walking all around me, but I can't seem to move. I'm embarrassed people will see me watching, but then again, everyone else is, too.

"Good evening, I'm Trent. Would you like a drink?" Clearing my throat, I look over to see a young guy with platinum hair and a bright smile. He has to be in his early twenties. "Um, can I have a water?"

"Sure," he replies, his smile growing wider.

There's an empty table toward the back of the room and that's exactly where I go. Women are everywhere, including several men gawking at the strippers on stage. Trent comes back with a bottle of water and hands it to me. "Enjoy your night. I'll come back around in a few minutes to check on you."

I nod. "Thank you."

Once he's gone, another stripper takes the stage, wearing holey jeans and a white T-shirt. He has light brown hair and tanned skin, which looks good against his white shirt. His body moves across the stage as if he's born to be there. He slides down to the floor and thrusts like he's fucking the air. It's so hot I can feel my insides tighten. I want to reach between my legs and satisfy the ache. *Oh, the lustful sins going through my head right now.* All of my friends experimented with sex when we were in high school. I'm the only one who shied away from it. Now, it's like all of my desires and hidden cravings have come at me full force.

The stripper finishes on stage and joins the crowd of women, making his way through them with a huge smile on his face. The ladies go crazy, but none of them touch him. His gaze catches mine and I suck in a breath; especially, when he heads my way.

I don't want to talk to him.

Grabbing my bottle of water, I get up as fast as I can. I've seen enough. The door is only a few yards away, but before I can close the distance, a guy steps in front of me. "Hi," he says, his lips pulling back in a sexy smirk.

"Hi," I reply. His dark brown hair is gelled in messy spikes and he has bright blue eyes. He could easily be one of the strippers, but he's dressed in one of the tuxedos.

Holding out his hand, his eyes stay fixed on mine. "My name's Jared. You're Alexandria, right?"

I shake his hand. "How did you know that?"

He shrugs. "I know everyone in this room. I can also tell it's your first time here."

Cheeks flaming, I cover my face. "Oh, my God, is there a sign on my forehead? You're the second person to tell me that."

I slide my hands down my face and he laughs. "I've been in this business for a while now. If it makes you feel any better, there's a few newbies in this room tonight."

Glancing around the room, I can't tell who's who. "Were you getting ready to leave? I see you were headed for the door."

I shrug. "I don't know if I belong here. Don't get me wrong, it's an amazing club, but it's not my scene."

His brows furrow. "Sure about that? You haven't been here long. There are other parts of the club you haven't seen."

My pulse spikes and I can feel the sweat beading at my back. Dani and Adrienne told me about the sex rooms. "Don't you have to be a member to see those parts?" I ask.

"You do. That's why I'm here talking to you. I selected you to become a member if that's something that interests you."

"Really?" I gasp. "What do you get with a membership?"

His eyes twinkle in the lights. "Follow me and I'll show you." I look around the room and I can't help but notice a lot of evil glares as I follow Jared. He glances back and notices my hesitance. Grinning slyly, he nods toward one of the side doors. "They're looking at you like that because they know what I'm offering you."

He opens the door and it seals behind us. The hallway is long and dimly lit with several other closed doors. "I'm assuming you don't accept everyone?" I ask.

"Unfortunately, no. Not everyone meets our criteria." I follow him down the hall and he stops at one of the closed doors, his hand on the handle.

"Why did you pick me?"

He stares right into my eyes. "You have an innocence about you. It's what drew me to you in the first place. Being promiscuous isn't what all we search for. I watched you looking at the strippers. You like what you saw, but you're afraid to admit it."

It's like he can see right through me. "This is all new to me. I don't know what I'm doing."

"You're here," he says, his voice like smooth honey. "It's the first step." When he presses down on the door handle, the door slides open. It's dark inside, but he nods for me to take a peek. There's a couch straight ahead with a woman facing the stage and a man kneeling on the floor, his face buried between her legs. On the stage is a couple having sex, their moans loud enough for me to hear.

Placing a hand on my chest, I step back and Jared closes the door. "Oh, my God."

He chuckles lightly. "That's the viewing room. We have a lot of couples who like it. Instead of watching porno movies at home, they come here to watch it live. But you can watch anything you desire. It can be something as simple as a strip tease, or someone masturbating, or people having sex. There are a ton of people who love being watched."

I clear my throat. "It's very interesting." As much as I want to explore things for myself, that isn't one of them. I'm a little too modest.

Jared stops at another door but doesn't attempt to open it. "Inside here is the dark room. It's occupied right now. Basically, it's a place where you can have a partner and not ever have to know who they are. It's completely dark to keep anonymity."

"That's interesting as well," I say, unable to form any other words. The thought of the dark room intrigues me, but there's something no one knows other than my friends ... I'm a virgin.

Jared grins, clearly finding me amusing. "The last of our rooms is the play room." He walks down to the final door and opens it. It's a huge room with a bed, but there's a lot of empty space. "We're getting ready to set it up for our next clients. That's why there's nothing in here yet."

I step inside the room. "What do people do in here?"

Jared peers around the room and then back to me. "Anything you want. It's more like a fetish room. We have some clients who love sucking toes and other clients who love having their toes sucked. It works perfectly for them. There are even others who enjoy the simple things like blowjobs and breast massages. If you decide to join us, I'll be your club contact. If there's something you're interested in, you can tell me, and I'll match you up."

"What about my identity? How can you keep that hidden?"

"Simple," he says with a grin. "Your partners don't have to know who you are. If you want, we can make sure they're blindfolded. Whatever you want, we can do … within reason."

I walk over to the bed and slide my fingers across the silky, red fabric. The thought of lying on it while a man touches me makes my body tremble. "I'm not experienced, Jared. I wasn't kidding when I said I'm new to all of this."

"It's my job to pick out those who can do this, Alexandria. We all have desires and things we secretly want. For new female members, you get a month free to try everything out. After that, there'll be a membership fee. You and your partners will be able to rate the experiences you share with each other once they're done."

Eyes wide, I glance at him over my shoulder. "You mean, they can say if I'm good or not?" With my luck, I'll get a bad rating for not being sexy enough, or being completely clueless. If the workers here can see I'm a newbie, I have no doubt my partners will be able to as well.

He chuckles. "And you can do the same. If you want to be good, you'll have to practice. Not all of us were experts when we first started. Think of it as a learning experience."

Taking a deep breath, I close my eyes and slowly let the air out. "Okay," I blurt out. "I'm in. Where do I sign?"

FIVE

Kai

I sip on my rum and Coke while the woman in front of me dances slowly. Her dark hair is curled, leaving her long locks to spring with every step or movement she makes.

Her finger goes to her mouth. Her tongue darts out, wetting it before she simulates a blowjob. I grab my dick, letting her know exactly where her mouth can go, but she doesn't catch my drift.

She continues to saunter in front of me, bending to show me her voluptuous ass. I'm tempted to grab a hold of her hips and pull her to my face so I can taste her, every inch of her, but I refrain. I like this little game that she's playing.

Her hands snake behind her back as she looks at me from over her shoulder, tossing her hair at the same time. It'd look glorious threaded through my fingers. Knowing this excites me. I rub the front of my pants again, showing that with each teasing moment, she's making me harder and harder.

The clasps on her bra are undone and she pulls her shoulders forward, as if she's suddenly shy. Doesn't she know that she's here for me? That I came here to watch her? Fuck her? I hate this teasing shit and am about to tell her as much, except she turns around and shows me her tits. They're massive, more than a handful, but something I can definitely motorboat. I'm desperate to see her taut nipples, but her hair is in the way. I reach out to brush it aside, but she sidesteps out of my way.

She starts to dance and I lean forward to get a better look at her nipples. Only they're covered by fucking tassels. I throw my hands up in frustration, but she just shakes her head. This is all a game to her. Doesn't she understand that I need her? That my cock is aching to be sucked by her naughty mouth?

No, she doesn't because she continues to gyrate the air, as if the mother fucking air is the man that she wants to be with. Another rum and Coke appears. Thank fuck because I need it to quench my thirst. I sip it slowly, savoring the amber taste as it drips down the back of my throat. If I didn't know any better, I would think that she's intent on getting me drunk.

She comes back over, this time crawling toward me. When she's in front of me, she licks her lips and sits back on her knees, thrusting her breasts inches from my face. I reach for a tassel to pull it off, but it doesn't budge. It must be stuck with superglue or something because I've pulled those off before. Haven't I? I can't recall, but it seems like a normal thing to do.

My girl comes back toward me, teasing me with the thin straps of her thong. She pulls them out, away from her body, only to snap them back in place. She does this again and again, each time showing me a bit more of her pussy. I'm growing tired of her cat and mouse game. I want to get down to business. I'm a busy man and she knows this.

Standing, I rip the button of my slacks off, yank the

zipper down, and rub the front of my bulge. She licks her lips. Oh yeah, baby, two can play this game. My dick grows harder, begging to be let out from its cloth confines. Gripping the elastic waistband, I push my briefs down until they're resting around my knees.

My cock springs up, slapping against my skin. The woman crawls toward me, licking her lips as she does. She beckons me toward her, but I sit back down in the chair and start stroking myself.

She sits back and spreads her legs, pushing her thong aside. Her finger slides up and down her pussy, finally inserting two fingers deep inside of her core. I move my chair closer so I can get a better look and she does the same thing.

"Yeah, baby," I say as I tighten the hold on my dick. "Fuck those fingers."

She does as I command, rocking her hips back and forth. She looks fucking sexy up there and I need a better look. As I get closer, she lays back. My free hand spreads her leg out wider so I don't miss anything.

"I need ..." she mutters.

"What do you need?"

"This," she says as she sticks her foot into my mouth.

Foot. Toes. Toenails. Toe jam. Callous.

I start gagging and she moves her toes against my tongue. A nail jabs into the roof of my mouth. I try to pull away, but she only moves with me. I can't breathe, and feel my stomach starting to roll. I slap at her foot, but she only crams it harder down my throat.

My cheeks expand like I'm holding a gallon of water in my mouth, except it's not water. Everything from my stomach expels all over her foot, leg and pussy, none of it getting onto the floor.

Her eyes turn red as she roars, growing taller and taller

as she hovers over me. She reaches down and pulls my dick until it pops off. I cry out but she just laughs and disappears behind the door.

The lights come on. I look around and find everyone laughing at me. Slowly, I glance down at my crotch and find my dick missing. I'm not bleeding and it doesn't hurt. It's just that my dick doesn't exist anymore.

I startle awake, heart racing. What the fuck did I just dream about? My heart is racing in fear. My hands are at my side, pressing into the mattress. Sweat drips into my eyes, but I'm afraid to move to wipe it away. Hell, I'm afraid to move in case that woman is still somewhere in my room. Talk about a nightmare from hell.

My phone rings. It's not on my nightstand but in the other room. I try to move, but my muscles fight against me. My eyes adjust to the small sliver of light peeking through my blinds, but it's not enough for me to see around my room. I try to calm my heartbeat so I can hear what's going on in the living room, but aside from my ringing phone I don't hear anything else.

The last thing I remember is being with Parker and Bryant ... Bryant and that stupid fucking club.

"God, did I go there with him last night?" I finally move my hand to rub it over my face. My groin twitches. I'm hesitant to look under my covers, fearful that I did in fact lose my ... my stomach rolls as visions start replaying in my mind.

Toes. I remember sharp toes being crammed into my mouth. I hate toes and their unhealthy habits. I can't take it anymore. Throwing my comforter back, I turn until my feet are touching the hardwood floors.

Slowly, I look at my crotch. "Thank you, Jesus," I mutter as I see my morning wood peeking through the flap

32

of my boxers. I don't think I have ever been so excited to see my dick before.

My phone rings again, and this time I make my way into the living room to answer it.

"Hey, Mom."

"Kai, did I wake you?"

She knows she did. She called twice. "Nah, I couldn't find my phone."

"Oh, do you have a lady friend over? What's her name?" She sounds so excited.

"Um ..." Pausing with my mother is never a good thing.

"Oh no, we're you ... you know, giving her the nuts?" The woman's lost her damn mind. It must be all the romance novels she reads. My father loves it. He keeps saying I need to find a woman who likes to read. Apparently, their sex life is better because of it.

"Jesus Christ," I mutter. "There isn't anyone here, Mom. And if there were, I don't think I'd be calling it 'giving her the nuts.' I don't know where you heard that shit from."

She bursts out laughing. "Some of the ladies at work were calling it that. I thought it was the new trend. I won't call it that anymore."

"Thank you." I walk into the kitchen to start a pot of coffee. I need it after that fucked up dream.

"Are you even meeting any women out there?" she asks.

"Not yet. I've only been here for a few days. Give me time," I tell her.

"You know it's okay if you're gay. Your father and I will understand."

I shake my head. "I'm not gay, Mom. I will meet someone soon." I just chose not to tell her about all the

33

women I've slept with. Once my coffee's done, I pour myself a cup and sit down on the couch.

"How's your job? Is your boss being nice to you?"

"Of course. We're getting ready to start a huge project." Closing my eyes, I fall back onto my couch. I tell her everything that is going on, what I'm going to be doing for Sweet Briar. She tells me that her and my father will look it up and see if it's a place that she wants to visit. She never will. Every time I've moved, she's said the same thing, but always found a reason not to come visit. I get it, she's afraid to fly and the thought of driving doesn't appeal to her. Anything that isn't within thirty minutes of home is out of the way for her.

"Well, that's good sweetheart."

"How's dad?" I ask, finishing up my coffee. I hurry into my bedroom to get ready for the day. My mother can talk for hours on the phone if I let her. She's funny as hell though.

She sighs. "Not too bad. He has to have a colonoscopy next week. That's what happens when you get old."

"I see that. Tell him I hope it goes okay."

"Oh, I will. And just so you know, I read a study on the prostate the other day. It said that to avoid issues, make sure to have sex frequently. If you don't have a partner, then take matters into your own hands ... literally." She giggles and I shake my head. I thank any deity that is listening that she is saying this over the phone and not out loud in front of a bunch of people. Whose mother reminds them to jack off frequently to keep their prostate healthy? Mine does as if it's an everyday conversation to have with your son.

When she finally hangs up, I stay where I am and analyze my dream. If I hadn't been to that club, I wouldn't have had that nightmare.

Feet.

In my mouth.

The thought makes me want to hurl.

I rush to the bathroom and quickly brush my teeth. I don't care if I it was a dream. I can still feel something in my mouth. After I thoroughly rinse out my mouth, I stare at myself in the mirror. I regret filling out that form, listing my fetishes. I have none. I have fears, and my nightmare played out my worst one.

I pray that I'm never called.

SIX

Alexandria

---

*W*hen I get off from work, I head to the gym.
It's been forever since I've gone. Adrienne
used to go with me until her pregnancy started wearing her
out. She doesn't have the energy after work anymore. I just
hate going by myself. Today, I'm sucking it up, and of
course, it's a packed house.

I walk inside and sign in before heading to one of the
stair climbers. The woman on the one beside me smiles and
continues with her workout. Slipping in my earbuds, I turn
on some Technotronic and move to the beat. The songs
make me want to dance, but I've always been a little clumsy.
Dancing on the stair climber will no doubt end in disaster.

Sweat pours down my back and my legs begin to burn.
At least, now, I won't feel so bad when I eat a bowl of ice
cream later. My phone rings and I don't recognize the
number. I'm out of breath, but I pull out my earbuds and
answer the phone.

"Hello?"

"Alexandria, this is Jared from Society X. How
are you?"

I gasp and look around, hoping like hell the woman beside me couldn't hear. "Yes, hi. I'm doing good. You?" Grabbing my bottle of water, I hurry off the stair climber to a vacant corner across the room.

"Can't complain. I'm calling because I have a proposition you might be interested in. You put in your application that you're open to anything. Is that correct?"

My cheeks burn like fire. "Yeah, I guess so. What exactly is this proposition?"

He clears his throat. "I have a client who has particular tastes, or fetishes if you prefer. His partner can't make it tonight, and I need to fill that spot."

Swallowing hard, my heart races. I'm nervous just hearing him talk about it. "What will I have to do?"

"You, absolutely nothing. All you'll have to do is lie there on your stomach while your partner massages your backside."

"You mean my back?" I ask.

He clears his throat again. "No, your ass."

I don't know what comes over me, but I burst out laughing. "You're joking, right?"

"No, I'm not."

I hush up quickly. "I honestly didn't know that was a thing. It's an interesting concept."

"Is it something you'd be interested in? You don't have to be naked. Your upper body will be covered by a curtain so you can wear a shirt. However, below your waist, you'll need to wear a thong."

Keeping a straight face and not laughing is going to be the hardest part of the whole thing. How can someone get off by rubbing someone's ass? "Sure, put me down. What time do I need to be there?" I say it before even really thinking it through.

"Eight o'clock. I'll see you then," Jared says.

"All right."

We hang up, and I head straight for the gym door. There's no way I can keep something like that a secret from my friends. Once outside, I call Dani.

"What's up, girl?"

I rush to my car and hop inside. "You will not believe the phone call I just got."

"What's going on?"

I haven't told her about being a member of Society X yet. "I kind of became a member of Society X."

"Holy shit," she squeals. "Seriously? Why didn't you tell me at work today?"

Sighing, I pull out of the parking lot for home. "Honestly, I didn't think I'd get a request so fast. My contact called me and said he had a proposition for me. And get this, it's for the play room. The guy wants to massage my ass."

Dani's cackle is so loud I have to hold the phone away from my ear. "That's priceless. Please tell me you said yes."

I groan. "Unfortunately. What if I burst out laughing while this dude's squeezing my butt cheeks?"

Dani's laughing so hard I'm surprised she can even breathe. "I don't know what to say. This is too funny. What kind of freak gets off on someone's ass?"

"Obviously, the man I'm about to give my ass to." I'm starting to think I made a mistake accepting the proposition. At least, I'll have a good story to tell later. "Wish me luck."

"Good luck, chickee. I want all the details."

On the way home, I glance at myself in the mirror. *What the hell am I doing?*

~

I EAT dinner when I get home and change clothes before going to the club, making sure to put on a nice, black thong. When I get to the front, I go through security and Jared is right there, waiting for me, dressed in his perfectly tailored tux.

"Good evening, Alexandria. Thank you for coming on such short notice." He grins, and a part of me wonders how he can even keep his composure knowing I'm about to get my ass massaged.

"No problem," I reply, following him to a side door. Everyone else is going through the main entrance which leads to the stripper rooms.

Jared unlocks the door and we walk down the long hallway until we get to the end. He leads me into a small room that's connected to the play room and opens the door to it. I can see the bed and a curtain covering half of it.

Jared points to the bed. "You'll lie on there to where your top half will be covered. Your partner will not see you and he won't talk."

"How long is this going to last?" I inquire nervously. I don't want to be in there for hours while a man rubs my butt.

"We allow thirty minutes, but sometimes it's less. I can assure you it won't be any longer than thirty." Silently, I breathe a sigh of relief. I don't know if I can keep from laughing that long, or being completely creeped out. "When it's over, your partner will leave first."

"Got it," I tell him.

He smiles one more time. "I'll be in here waiting for you when it's done." He shuts the door behind him and I'm left alone in the changing room. After sliding my jeans down, I enter the play room. The bed looks comfortable and when I lie down, the silky sheets are cold against my thighs. The curtain surrounds me and I can't see anything outside of them. It's not long before the sound of a door opens and footsteps approach.

I try my best not to clench my butt cheeks, but it's hard not to. A satisfied moan escapes my partner's lips. He squeezes my ass and his breath hitches as if it turns him on. I bite my lip to keep from laughing. If I ruin his play time, they might not let me come back.

Another moan and the squeezing becomes faster, more intense. To be honest, it does feel good on my lower back. *Maybe it's not so bad after all.* That's what I tell myself until one of his hands disappears and more groaning ensues, followed by the sound of him jacking off. It's all so strange and I find it fascinating. How can anyone be turned on by someone's ass? I hold my breath so I can hear it all. The grunting stops and both hands touch my ass again, but his breaths are guttural and deep, like he's possessed.

He massages me some more, and then his hand slides off so he can finish masturbating. The sounds grow louder and I'm almost afraid he's going to tear his dick off. As long as he doesn't try to stick a finger up my ass, we're fine. His grunts finally come to an end and his fingers gently slither down my backside. He kisses my ass cheek and smacks it play-fully, moaning with delight. Closing my eyes, I wait desperately for the sound of the door to signal his departure. When I hear it click shut, I bury my face in the bed and laugh. I can't wait to tell Dani and Adrienne. All I know is I'm never agreeing to volunteer for that again.

SEVEN

Kai

_____

*T*he bulldozer cuts into the ground among very few onlookers. To my left is the town pastor, and to my right the self-dubbed mayor of Sweet Briar, Stan Mercer.

"It would've been nice to have a ribbon cutting ceremony," Stan says. His arms are crossed, causing the fabric in his sport coat to stretch. "Invite the news out, have a bar-be-cue."

"In due time," I tell him. "Once the apartments are up, we'll have a massive celebration and I'll make sure to bring those giant scissors so you can cut the ribbon." I'm mentally shaking my head, but I get it. Mayors like to be on television. They want their people to see that they're doing well in their community.

Except right now, Mayor Stan isn't doing anything. Parker and Larry are. If it weren't for these two men, the bulldozer a few yards in front of me wouldn't be cutting into the land to prepare it for a foundation.

While Stan continues to yammer on to Larry about how we missed an opportunity by not having the news here, I meet with the construction manager. The mobile office, which is a fancy business term for trailer, is unstable and rickety. It wobbles when I step into the makeshift office.

"Hello, Mr. Robicheau."

"Hi ..."

"Brenda," the receptionist says. She gives me a small wave, which I have a feeling is meant to be flirtatious.

"Right, hi." Bypassing her, I walk past the imaginary wall where Greg Parsons is bent over a drafting table. "You missed it," I tell him, sitting down in his chair. I make the mistake of glancing up and find Brenda staring at me. I offer her a quick smile and turn my attention toward Greg's back. It's much more entertaining than trying to ignore his assistant.

"Sorry, I'm trying to make sure that everything is set for tomorrow," Greg says.

"You think they'll be ready to pour concrete tomorrow?"

Greg lifts the slat of the blinds. His head moves from side to side, as if he's trying to see around the corner. "We are working from sunup to sundown. We'll be pouring by the end of the week."

"That's what I like to ..." My train of thought is interrupted by a text alert.

Mr. Robicheau, this is Jenica from Society X. We have a match for you. Please let me know if you're free this evening.

I shake my head and slip my phone back into my pocket. "I'm going to kill him," I mutter under my breath. Greg looks at me curiously. "I need to head back to Portland and finalize some contracts. I'll be back in the morning, but if you need me, call."

"Will do, boss."

I make the mistake of looking at Brenda as I pass by. She finger waves, to go along with the widest, and almost scariest smile I have ever seen. Thing is, she's a pretty woman, but trying too hard and that is a turn off. "See ya later," I tell her as I step out of the trailer and out onto the job site. For a minute, I take in all that is happening.

Multiple bulldozers are breaking land, digging into the earth so we can pour the necessary concrete foundation for the apartments. By the end of the week, footings should be in place and concrete poured. I plan to be here for that.

Off to the side, trees are being taken down to make room for the parking lot, playground, and swimming pool. For every tree we're taking down, two are being planted. We're also planting a community garden. Not only will it give residents a chance to grow their own, but to feed their less fortunate neighbors.

In my mind, I can see this project taking shape, and it's just the start at bringing life back to Sweet Briar.

The text alert on my phone chimes again as I get into my car. It's that woman, Jenica, from the sex club. This time I don't even look at what she has to say because my answer will still be no. I have never been desperate enough to seek out attention in the paid form. I don't care if I'm new the city, I can get laid whenever I want. In fact, I can probably go back and take Brenda out, but I have a strict policy against screwing co-workers. Nothing good ever comes from hooking up with people you work with.

The traffic back to Portland is heavy and somewhat frustrating. Every time my phone chimes, all I can think about is Jenica telling me that there's a match for me. The thought terrifies me to no end considering I filled out the application with nothing but lies. While I like a little freak in the bedroom, I'd have to say my tastes are very vanilla and that isn't what I put on the application. No, my dumbass had to put down that I'm into fetishes, that I like sucking on toes or having mine sucked on. The last thing I want is for a woman to touch my feet.

When my phone rings, I press the hands-free button without looking at the caller identification.

"Kai here," I say loudly due to the top of my car being down.

"Mr. Robicheau, this is Jenica. Have I caught you at a bad time?"

"No. I don't know."

"I know you're busy so I'll cut to the chase. I don't know if you saw my texts earlier, but I wanted to let you know that we have a match for you. She would like to meet you tonight, if you're free, for a blowjob."

I look around, wondering who can hear her. There are other people talking animatedly in their cars. Music blares from others. "Um ... is this a joke? Did Bryant put you up to this?"

"I assure you that I'm serious, Mr. Robicheau. Society X takes their clients' needs very seriously."

"Right. So I get a blowjob and she gets what in return? I mean, am I obligated to you ... you know ..." I can't bring myself to saying the action out loud. Don't get me wrong, I'm all for eating some pussy, but I'd like to know the woman first, get a sense on whether she's clean or not.

"The request is for a blowjob to take place in the play room. There isn't any other indication that the client would like anything else."

"That just doesn't make sense," I tell her as I move along with the traffic. "Every woman I know wants something in return."

"I'm sorry, Mr. Robicheau, but that doesn't seem to be the case this time."

Sighing loudly, I continue to look around to see if anyone is listening in on my conversation, not that I expect that they can hear me. "So you're telling me that I show up at the club, drop my pants to my knees, and let some chick suck my dick?"

"Yes, that is what the client has requested."

And because my dick has been at full attention since our encounter in Society X, he perks up. "Stupid fucker," I mutter.

"Excuse me?"

"Sorry, not you," I tell Jenica. "Look, I'll try it this one time, but I really don't think I'm the kind of guy who does this type of stuff."

"Of course. I completely understand. I will text you the information." She hangs up, and just like that I have an appointment at the sex club, all thanks to that fucker Bryant. I'm tempted to ask him about the rooms, to find out exactly what happens in them, but I don't want him to think I'm interested, especially since he likes to eat "lunch" there.

By the time I reach the office I am completely frazzled. I can't think. My semi won't calm down. And all I can imagine in my mind is some woman on her knees, sucking my dick. Of course, when I think about that, my dick starts dancing in my pants.

Jenica sends me a text with the time that I need to arrive. I stare at my phone, tempted to tell her I've changed my mind, that this is something I can't do. I need to have a stimulating conversation with someone before I stick my dick in their mouth.

What if I can't get it up? What if when she touches me I go limp? The pressure to perform is too great. I pick up my phone and type out the words, telling Jenica thanks, but no thanks ... only I can't bring myself to press the send button.

"Fucking Bryant," I say loud enough to fill the silence in my office. "Fuck it." I grab my stuff and quickly head out of the office, hoping to avoid running into Parker or Bryant. I don't want to lie to Parker as to why I'm leaving early, and if I see Bryant, I might strangle him for putting me in this position.

I rush home and head straight for the shower. I leave my hard-on alone, afraid that if I get myself off now, I won't be able to get it up for the woman who wants to suck me off. Just the thought of getting a blowjob makes me harder.

"What the fuck am I doing?" I ask myself loudly as I stare down at my dick. "Going to go get a blowjob," I say as I shut the water off.

After drying off, I dress as casually as possible. As luck would have it, the drive to Society X takes me ten minutes. It was my hope that I'd be late and my appointment would be canceled. But no, here I am and there's Jenica, waiting for me.

"Follow me," she says as she punches a code into the panel. The door opens and closes almost as soon as I step over the threshold. "As I said, you'll be in the play room." She adds another code and the door opens.

The room is bare, other than a chair and what looks like a thick, black curtain. "You'll sit on the chair, with the rest of your body behind the curtain. You are not allowed to speak or look at the woman."

"Why not?"

"Because at Society X, everything is anonymous. She won't look at you or even speak. When you're done, you'll rate her, as she will rate you."

Great!

"Okay, so I just sit there?"

"Yes. When she's done, she will leave first. I will knock once to let you know it's time for you come out. You have one minute to be ready."

Jenica leaves, and I find myself standing in the middle of this room with a chair that looks intimidating as fuck. I go over to it and undo my pants, letting them drop to the ground, and sit down and make sure that I'm hidden behind the curtain.

The door opens and there's an audible gasp. Right off, I'm self-conscious, wondering if she thinks I'm too small.

Fuck. Gripping my shaft, I move my hand up and down, praying that this fucker gets bigger for her. I jump slightly when her hands touch my knees and stop my self-pumping action.

The first lick has my dick twitching away from her in reaction, but she doesn't hesitate. She licks the head again and again, pausing for a few seconds before wrapping those lips of hers around the tip of my cock. She takes me deep into her mouth and slowly pulls away, only to do it again and again.

Her hand grips my dick and pumps in sequence with her mouth, creating a vacuum of suction that almost has me coming, but I fight it. I think about granny panties and Bryant—that stupid fucker. When she moans, my hand instantly threads through her hair and my hips thrust.

She works my cock down the back of her throat. Right now, I want to say, "Fuck it," toss this curtain aside, and bury my dick deep into her pussy. When she starts to massage my balls, my eyes roll back in my head and I mutter, "Fuck yes," breaking one of the rules.

EIGHT

Alexandria

---

*W*hen I walk into the room, I have no clue what to expect. There's a curtain in place with a man sitting behind it, his bare legs and cock on full display. It's definitely different from the other night when I had to lie on a bed and get my ass massaged. *What the hell was I thinking agreeing to let that happen?* There was nothing stimulating about it. This, however, is a different story.

The scent of his expensive cologne wafts in the air and I breathe him in. He smells so damn good. Kneeling down between his legs, I try to remember everything from the porno videos I watched the night before. Never in my life would I have considered watching a porno, but I needed the help. I've watched videos on how to jack a guy off, massage his balls, and how to suck it just right. I'm not like everyone else I know who've had multiple partners and know what they're doing.

For a tiny moment, I can't help but stare at the man's body. His dick is so large and hard, it's intimidating. I'm so afraid I'll gag if I take him too far down my throat. Taking a deep breath, I wrap my lips around the tip and slowly take him into my mouth. He tastes salty and I swallow it down. When I hear the man's groans of satisfaction, I suck him harder, wrapping my hands around the base of his cock so I can pump him.

The second I start massaging his balls, that's when I hear him say, "Fuck yes," in a voice so deep and sexy, I want to hear more of it. The sound sends shivers down my arm, but then, I realize, he's just broken one of the rules.

He moans even more and I'm hoping it means I'm doing something right. He fists his hands in my hair and it's my turn to gasp. Just the thought of pleasing him turns me on. I've never had much confidence when it came to men, but right now, it feels like I can do anything. It's nice being desired, even if he doesn't know who I am.

Closing my eyes, I take him down farther, squeezing my mouth against him as hard as I can. My cheek muscles burn, but I can't stop. The insides of my legs are drenched and I'm aching to feel a release. I never would've thought I'd be turned on by sucking a man's dick. It makes me want so much more.

The faster I pump and suck him, the louder his moans grow. His cock hardens even more and I can feel it pulsating against my lips. "I'm going to come," he says with a groan. "You might want to move away."

My eyes snap open and I pull away, his hands sliding through my hair as the warm, milky liquid of his release shoots out of his cock. It gets all over the back of my hand and I don't know what to do with it so I wipe it on his leg. Maybe it *was* a good idea to pull away instead of swallowing it all. I probably would've choked with how much came out.

"You're not supposed to talk," I whisper low.

He chuckles. "Just trying to be considerate. Most women don't like to swallow."

Rising to my feet, I step back toward the door. "Thanks. I hope you enjoyed it."

"You were amazing," he murmurs huskily. "Maybe one day you'll let me return the favor." It's strange talking to a man who's behind a curtain. A part of me just wants to tear it back and see who he is, but then again, not knowing is very intriguing.

I stop at the door, wishing he could help ease the ache between my legs. "We'll see."

A deep chuckle escapes his lips again, almost like he knows it'll happen one way or another. I quickly open the door and shut it behind me. Jared is waiting for me with a smile on his face. "How'd it go?"

Heat rises to my cheeks. "Good," is all I can say.

He hands me a long, black box and steps back. "Welcome to Society X, Alexandria."

A part of me wants to come back so bad I can taste it, but the other part, can't help but feel like it's wrong to want such carnal pleasures. Especially, with men I have no connection with. I open the box and inside there's an exquisite silver necklace with a diamond encrusted charm in the shape of an X.

"The next time you come, make sure you wear that around your neck," Jared instructs.

I stare at the necklace and then close the box. "Thank you. It's very beautiful."

"Shall I put you on the schedule again? Maybe even try a different room?"

My cheeks burn when I meet his gaze. "Not yet. I need to process this all first."

He nods and guides me to the back door. "I understand. Whenever you're ready, just give me a call. I already emailed a survey to you about your partner. All I need you to do is fill it out as soon as you can."

The door opens and I step out into the cool, night air. "And he gets to do the same?" I ask, peering at him over my shoulder.

Jared grins. "He does. And if you ever want the same partner again, we can make it happen."

"Thanks. I'll be in touch." Turning my back, I walk to my car with a smile on my face. Once inside, I pull out my phone and bring up my email. The survey is there and I fill it out, giving my partner an excellent review. All I have to do now is wait to see what he says about me.

THE NEXT MORNING, I get up and prepare for work. My Society X necklace is secure around my neck, hidden beneath my shirt. It feels sexy and sinful having it on, hiding it so no one can see. I open my front door and stop when my phone beeps with an incoming email. Holding my breath, I freeze where I stand. I glance down at the screen and it's from Society X with the results of my rating.

My heart pounds in my chest. I'm nervous and excited, but also terrified. What if the man ends up giving me a bad rating? If so, I know I'll never show my face around the club again. Impatience overtakes me and I open the email, not caring that my door is wide open behind me. I can't wait another second longer.

The email is splayed on my screen but I close my eyes and take a deep breath. I don't even know why I care so much. Opening my eyes, I stare down at my results. Excitement bubbles in my chest and I burst out laughing. The man gave me all good ratings, and even put yes as the answer to the question on if he wants to be with me again. My neighbor stops at the end of his driveway and stares at me as he's picking up the newspaper.

I lock my door and wave. "Good morning, Mr. Santiago."

Dressed in a pair of striped pajama pants with his gray hair in disarray, he waves back. Mr. Santiago is a nice man with an even nicer wife. Every time she makes cinnamon raisin bread, she always brings me a loaf. "Morning, Alexandria. You're awfully happy this morning."

I hurry to my car and throw my purse inside. "It's going to be a good day. Tell Mrs. Santiago I said hi."

"I will."

Getting in my car, I wave at him again and hurry to work. Sandy is there, preparing three whole trays of her buttermilk biscuits when I walk in the door. "Good morning, Alex. Did you have a good night?" she inquires.

Cheeks burning, I put on my apron and smile. "Yes, I did. You?"

She cuts the last of her dough and places the round pieces on the tray. "I did. The hubby and I went over to our daughter's house to eat dinner. I love seeing my grandbabies."

"And I bet they love seeing their nana." I walk over and start putting the trays of biscuits into the ovens. "What are we doing today?" There's always some kind of event we have to cater for, even if it's a large corporate event or a small meal for the local doctor's offices.

Sandy washes her hands, sighing. "The dentist office down the street called as soon as I came in, asking if we could make a huge breakfast for their employees. I figured we could get it done fast. We have an hour and a half before we have to deliver it."

Glancing at the clock, I smile. "We'll get it done." Breakfast is easy to make, especially, with four of us putting it together. Dani walks in and Adrienne follows behind her.

Sandy's gaze narrows at me. "You're chipper this morning. Dating someone?"

I burst out laughing. "Not exactly. Let's just say I had a good night." As soon as I got home from Society X, I took care of business to ease the ache between my legs. It felt so good I got off twice.

Dani and Adrienne stare at me and Dani snickers. Once Sandy walks out of the room, Dani and Adrienne both flank me as I crack the eggs. "Did you go to the club last night again?" Dani asks.

"Shh, don't talk so loud." Laughing, I shake my head.

"You did, didn't you? How'd it go? It wasn't like last time was it, with Mr. Butt Massager?" Adrienne asks, moving closer.

Giggling, I finish cracking the eggs and lean against the counter. "Hell, no. This time, it was exhilarating. Just being in the club is a high all in itself."

Dani nods. "That's what my cousin says all the time. She's addicted to that place."

Adrienne nudges me in the side. "Did you go in the same room?"

I smile at them. "Yep."

Dani fans herself. "Whoa, I bet that was hot. I think I need to give this place a try."

"What did you do in there?" Adrienne asks.

Biting my lip, I cover my face. "I gave a man a blowjob."

I peeked at her through my fingers, embarrassed even admitting it. "I wanted to see what it was like. And I didn't have to worry about the man watching me."

They both burst out laughing and Dani pats my shoulder. "Did you spit or swallow?"

"Actually, this is the interesting part. The guy warned me to back up and ended up coming all over himself."

Dani's eyes widen in disbelief. "Really? I didn't think you were allowed to talk in the rooms."

I shrug. "You're not, but I have to say, his voice was sexy as hell."

"Must be nice that he warned you to move away. Most men would make the girl swallow," Adrienne says, snorting in disgust.

Dani claps her hands excitedly. "Oh my God, do you think you'll go back and be with him again?"

Adrienne grabs my arm. "What if this guy's disgusting and fat with a beer gut?"

I shake my head. "His legs were athletic and slim. There's no way."

"I say go back and get your own pleasures," Dani suggests. "Might as well enjoy it."

Adrienne agrees with a nod. "Like she said. I'm living vicariously through you, my friend. I want to hear everything. It's better than a romance novel."

Groaning, I run my hands over my face. "Fine, I'll see what I can do. If this guy wants to be with me again, he has to make the first move."

Dani giggles. "Make him work for it, girl. You can always get another man to pleasure you."

I can, but deep down that's not what I want. "I think I'll wait it out," I say. "There's something about this guy I can't ignore. I want to know more about him. Maybe it's his voice, I don't know. I can't stop thinking about him."

Adrienne fans herself. "This is so hot."

My whole body is on fire. "Yes, it is. I just hope he wants to be with me again. After all, he did say he'd like to return the favor."

NINE

Kai

$\mathcal{T}$he world is evil. Actually, the man who created Society X is. All the time I've lived in California, not once had I stepped foot into a sex club. The horror stories I've heard about those places were enough to keep me satisfied with dating sites or meeting someone the old-fashioned way—in a bar.

And yet, here I am, sitting on the edge of my bed trying to imagine what the woman with the glorious mouth looked like. What colors are her eyes? Her hair? And why didn't I pull a strand when I had my fingers threaded into her mane? Because that would've been fucking creepy and that's not me.

I broke the rules. I didn't even hesitate to tell her that I was about to blow. I didn't want her to be grossed out or unprepared so I had to tell her. I'm sure that the club has video monitors and they know that I've violated the contract, on the first day no less.

Her voice is all I heard last night in my dreams. I had multiple dreams about her. She was a blonde, then a brunette, and a redhead. Her eyes were green, then blue, and brown. Each time she had the fullest lips and her smile was always the same. She'd wipe her mouth using just her index finger while she smirked at me, knowing full well that I'd be hard for her within seconds of her finishing me off.

And I was. The entire drive back to my place my cock ached for attention, demanding that I find him pleasure or take care of the deed myself. Let me tell you there is no amount of jacking off that curbs the desires left behind in the play room. I wanted carnal knowledge of the woman on her knees. Hot, uninhibited sex.

I head to the gym. I don't drive, but run, building up a sweat by the time I walk in. The music is pumping, weights clanking together and ass ... nothing but voluptuous, toned asses bouncing up and down while these gorgeous women run on the treadmills. That can't be me today, running along the side of them, not in my condition.

Instead, I head for the weights, praying that my erection subsides so that I don't hurt myself or cause any alarm to the body builders who can crush me with their bicep. Thankfully, it's me and another guy, and by the looks of him, he seems to be in the same boat I am. Each time he finishes a rep, he looks around. When one of the female trainers comes by, he frantically starts to pump iron.

He reminds me of Bryant in an odd sort of way. I have no idea if Bryant frequents Society X because he needs attention or longs for the company of a beautiful woman. What I don't understand is why. Bryant seems like a nice man and he has a good job. Those are two qualities that usually earn a man a date. But he prefers to visit the club, which is likely a turn off for most women.

After a few reps on the machines, I hit the sauna. I still

have time before I have to be in Sweet Briar. Thankfully, I'm the only one in here at this hour and I decide to let it all hang out. I'm man spreading and naked as the day I was born when the door opens. I cover up as quickly as possible, but it's still not enough. My only saving grace is that it's not overly bright in here and the steam adds a nice cloak.

Except the woman who entered the sauna has chosen to sit next to me. I tell myself to play it cool, and adjust as coyly as possible without drawing *that* much attention to myself. I cough and sort of slide/stand to fix my towel, and that is when I notice *it*. It being the X necklace women are given when they're members of Society X. I was given a leather bracelet, but there is no way in hell I'll wear it in public.

Yet, here is this women with her brunette hair pulled into a bun on the top of her head. Her eyes are closed so she can't tell that I'm looking at her ... chest.

"Hi," I say in the most awkward tone of voice I can imagine. I must pique her attention because she opens her eyes and smiles. That's right, she's smiling at me.

"Hey," she replies rather loudly.

Would it be creepy of me to ask her to whisper to me? Probably, right? "Uh, nice necklace."

She picks it up and her face pales. "Shit," she mumbles.

"Hey, it's okay. I'm a member, too."

"Really? Are you some fucking sicko? We're supposed to be anonymous and ... what the hell?" Her gaze lands on my hard dick. "Is that a fucking erection? Are you hard for me right now? You're fucking sick."

Before I can even utter an apology or ... hell, I don't know, save face, she storms out of the sauna. I glance down at the head of my dick, pointing out of the towel. The only thing he's not doing is waving a fucking flag telling everyone he's open for business.

Banging my head against the wall, I curse myself out. What a fucking moron I am, breaking yet another rule. I'm pretty certain she isn't the one I was with last night because the tone of her voice is way off. The mouth that was on me was sweet and shy. There's no way in hell that psycho bitch was sucking me off.

And if she was, I think she would've acted a bit differently at seeing my dick since she had him eye level for a good half hour.

The door opens again and I scramble to make sure my towel is covering my junk. I don't need any more random fuck ups, and I definitely don't need to be thrown out of the club.

"Ah, hey man," Bryant says as he sits down. He isn't shy about letting his shit hang out. I'm trying not to stare, but damn, man, I work with this guy and know everything there is to know about him. He loves titty bars and free balling. Fucking wonderful.

"Um ... how's it going?"

"Great. Man, I love the sauna."

"Yeah, me too." Just not with another guy next to me.

"Given any thought about checking out that club I took you to the other day?" he asks.

I shake my head. "Nah, I'm sort of busy and all. You?" I can't believe I just asked him if he's been. I do not care!

"You really need to see about being a member."

"I gotta tell ya, Bryant, titty bars aren't my thing," I say honestly.

"There's more than tits and ass. You see, Society X is this magnificent club where you can live out your fantasies and no one has to know about it. I saw you talking with one of the hostesses."

I nod, because there's no denying it.

"The fee is steep, but worth it. Last night I was in the dark room banging some chick. That has to be my favorite, although when I'm really wanting to get my freak on, I go to the viewing room."

Well, let's add this to shit that I don't need to know about Bryant. All I can do is nod and play along. Even if I were trying to recruit someone to join, I wouldn't tell him about my escapades. That should remain private.

"We should get lunch there today," Bryant says.

"By lunch you mean—"

"Lap dance or you can book a room and feast on pussy."

"Right. I'll be in Sweet Briar," I tell him. "Maybe we can grab lunch next week ... at a restaurant?"

"Yeah, sure."

"I'm going to go and beat traffic. See ya." I'm up and out of the sauna as fast as I can move. Of course, I'm back to sporting a fucking hard on because now all I can think about is returning the favor from last night. God, what I wouldn't give to feel her fingers in my hair. To make her moan, to feel her body quiver by the way I work her core.

Fuck my life.

After a quick shower, I pull my phone out of my locker and text Jenica.

Tonight? Same room, if possible? Same woman? I want to return the favor.

I knew I was getting a blowjob, so maybe if she knows that I want to show her the same pleasure that she's shown me, she'll want to meet me.

Instead of walking home, I hail a cab, and hold my phone in my hand until I have to set it down to get dressed. I don't know if I should text Jenica again. I mean, what's the appropriate amount of time to wait when soliciting oral sex?

Jesus Christ, even as I think that I'm asking myself, *What the fuck am I doing?* This isn't me ... but the thrill of it all is so exhilarating. There's a part of me that likes I don't know what she looks like, or her me. My body is actually craving the mystique behind it all, the secrecy. I can use my imagination and try things that I'd be too afraid to try if I could see her expression.

I pick my phone back up and text Jenica again.

And I want to be able to touch and massage her breasts.

Because I do. I love grabbing hold of a set of tits and burying my face deep in pussy. And I hope she slams her hand down on my head and holds me pressed against her. The shitty part is that I can't hear what she wants. She won't able to tell me that she's close or that she likes what I'm doing.

That's when it hits me. This club isn't about sex ... well it is, but not like the clubs in Los Angeles where people just go to fuck. This club is about people discovering how to communicate with their senses. It'll be my job to bring her pleasure, which means I have to watch her body for signs, I have to feel my way to her pleasure points.

What a crafty fucker this owner is, and now that I've realized this I'm pissed that I didn't think of the concept. I bring the club's website up and look around. It's basic with operating hours and a description of the exclusive rooms. You know it's expensive when it says call for rates, but something tells me that I won't mind paying for my membership.

Now begs the question. How far am I willing to go? Honestly, I want to test out all the rooms. I want to heighten my senses, but I don't want to go at it alone.

TEN

Alexandria

"*A*re you sure you don't need me anymore today?" I ask, wiping down the counters.

She waves me off. "I'm good. You and Dani came in early and worked through lunch. There's nothing else that needs to be done. Adrienne's really sick, so she'll probably be out tomorrow as well. I'll need you on your toes, so go get some rest."

Dani and I look at each other and smile. I grab my purse and the box of quiches I put aside for my mother. "Then, in that case, I'm out." I glance down at my watch. "Since it's early, I might go ahead and visit my mother."

"Tell your mom I said hi, and that I hope she's getting better," Sandy says as I walk out the door.

"I will," I call out.

Dani follows me out to the parking lot. "How's your mom doing anyway? Didn't she have surgery on her foot."

Opening my car door, I toss my purse inside. "Yeah, about five weeks ago. She's getting around better now. I think she goes back to work in another three weeks. I know she gets bored being at home all day by herself while my father works."

"I'd love having eight weeks off of work. I can read as many books as I want and drink wine all day." Smiling, she puts on her sunglasses.

"Nice," I laugh. "But I wouldn't want to have the kind of surgery she had. It's supposed to be really painful." Plus, I like cooking for a living. Not many people can say they love their job, but I do. I'm pretty sure I'll love it even more when I finally open up my own business.

Dani waves her hand in the air. "See ya tomorrow, girlie. Have a good night."

"You too."

I get in my car and head out of town to the small town of Sweet Briar. When I pull into the city limits, I can smell the salty sea air. Living by the coast was one of my favorite things as a child. Sweet Briar is like one of those small towns you'd see on TV where everyone has the white picket fences and knows their neighbors. I left it a couple of years ago to get more perspective on life. My parents are old-fashioned and were a tad bit strict on me growing up. It was mainly my dad. My mother was the one who was more lenient. I wasn't allowed to go on dates until I was eighteen years old. Guess you can say I didn't have many boyfriends in high school. When I went to college, I loved having the freedom of being away from home. That's why I haven't left Portland.

I turn down my parents' street and pull into the driveway of the home I grew up in. The siding is a light blue with white shutters around the windows and a white front door. The landscape is perfectly trimmed and the bushes are shaped to perfection. That's my father for you. He's the epitome of perfect. It's how I had to be growing up. It was exhausting.

By the time I'm out of my car, my mother already has the front door open. Her chocolate-colored hair is pulled high in a bun and she's wearing her favorite plaid pajama pants. "It's about time you come to visit me," she hollers teasingly. Laughing, I sling my purse around my shoulders and walk toward her, arms open. I hug her tight and she rubs my back. "You're here early. Did you not have to work?"

She lets me go and I walk into the house. "Sandy didn't need me anymore, so she gave me the rest of the day off. I thought I'd go ahead and come out here so we can spend more time together." The house smells like meatloaf and my mouth waters.

After shutting the door, my mom limps into the living room before plopping down on the couch. "Well, I'm glad you're here. I know it's not easy coming out here all the time. The traffic makes an hour drive turn into two sometimes."

I snort and sit down across from her. "Got that right. Today wasn't so bad. How's your foot?"

She turns off the TV and stretches her legs. "Much better. I'm allowed to put some weight on it now, but I'm scared to put too much. I have three more weeks to get better before I have to go back to work." She works at the local bank and stays on her feet all day. My father's been trying to get her to retire, but she loves working.

"What about Dad? Is he doing okay?"

A sad expression passes across her face and she nods. "He's fine. I know he misses you. Every time you come around, he's not here. I think he believes you're doing it on purpose."

Part of it's true, but I also have a life in Portland. It's hard for me to make the commute all the time. I wave her off. "I'm not doing it on purpose," I lie. "I can't help it he's never here when I come." His job is his life, it always has been. My whole childhood was based on trying to live up to his standards. Eventually, I got tired of it and stayed away once I started college. Pursing her lips, my mother stares at me, clearly not believing a single word I say. Clearing my throat, I nod toward the kitchen. "The meatloaf smells good. It's been months since I've had it."

"That's why I made an extra one so you can take it home. I know you usually make the fancy stuff at work."

She winks and I laugh. "My quiches are famous, Momma. One of these days, I'm hoping to have my own place." Sandy is getting older and I know she won't be able to keep up the catering business forever. Once she retires, I'll start up my own business so there's no competition.

"I'm sure you will, sweetheart," my mother says lovingly. As far as my dreams and goals in life, she's the one who's always had my back. "Have you started dating anyone?" Instantly, my face heats up and it's obvious she can see my reddening cheeks. "Oh, my gosh, you are, aren't you?"

"No," I blurt out. Visions of the play room and the man behind the curtain flashes through my mind. I can even hear his deep, seductive groans in my head. My whole body trembles and I clench my fists. *Shit.* I can't be thinking of those things with my mother right in front of me. "I guess you can say I had a date last night, but it's nothing serious." If she knew I spent the evening at Society X she'd have a heart attack. She probably doesn't even know what that place is. Living in Sweet Briar has sheltered her from the craziness of the big city life.

My mother beams. "If it gets serious, you need to bring him out here so I can meet him."

Nervously, I giggle and stand. "We'll see. I'm going to head to the bathroom really quick." I'm hoping my time away will make her forget about my dating life. Hurrying to the bathroom farthest away from the living room, I shut the door. My phone vibrates in my purse and I pull it out. I gasp when I see it's Jared from Society X. I clear my throat and press the answer button, keeping my voice low. "Hello."

"Alexandria, it's Jared. How are you?"

I listen for my mother, and thankfully, she's still in the living room laughing at something on the TV. "Good. And you?"

"Never better," he replies. "Listen, I'm calling because I need to know if you'd be interested in accepting a proposal for the play room. Your recent partner requested to meet you again. Is that something you're interested in?"

My body tingles in anticipation. "Sure," I answer without thinking it through. "What will we be doing in there?"

"Actually, *you* won't be doing anything. Your partner has requested to return the favor."

"How?" I ask breathlessly.

Jared coughs which almost sounds like an amused laugh. "You want the details?"

"Yes." My mind shifts to the play room. I want to imagine how it'll all go down.

"In that case, here you go. He wants to go down on you and make you come. He also wants permission to touch your breasts and everything below. All you're required to do is lie on the bed." A few seconds pass. "Is that something you want to do?"

"Yes," I blurt, feeling as if I'm going to explode. "I'll be there. Just name the time."

"Eight o'clock."

"Count me in."

"See you then, Alexandria." He hangs up and I'm left with a growing ache between my legs. My nipples pucker and rub against my shirt and all I want is to feel them squeezed by the strength of a man's hands. Slipping a hand up my shirt, I massage them hard, pinching my nipples between my fingers. It doesn't quench my thirst. I slide my other hand down my pants and the second I touch my throbbing clit, I know that's where I'm needed.

I rub my fingers over it, gently gliding two of my fingers inside of me. I bite my lip to hold in my pleasure-filled cries. My fingers are drenched, sliding in so easily with each thrust. I squeeze my breasts harder and rub my clit faster. My release comes quick and I fall back against the wall with a thud, gasping for air.

A knock sounds on the door and I suck in a breath. "Yeah?"

"You okay in there?" my mom asks.

Looking at myself in the mirror, I smile. "I'm perfect."

PULLING into the Society X parking lot makes me both nervous and excited. My necklace is on and I have a sexy set of pink lingerie on under my clothes. I'm ready to go, but I can't stop the butterflies in my stomach. I've dated men who wanted to go down on me, but I never let them. What's crazy is that I'm letting a complete stranger do it. Maybe it's because he doesn't know who I am and I don't have to feel embarrassed if I thrash around like an idiot. If touching myself gives me so much pleasure, I can only imagine what it'll feel like for a man to do it.

Taking a deep breath, I get out of my car and head for the entrance. Once inside, Jared is waiting for me with a smile on his face. "Ready?"

I swallow hard. "I think so."

He leads me to one of the small rooms connected to the play room. It's where he'll come get me once everything's said and done. He opens the door to the play room and nods inside. I look in to see a bed with a curtain draped over part of it. "When you're ready, lie on the bed to where your chest and below are exposed. Your partner will be in shortly."

I shiver in anticipation. "Sounds good. Thanks."

"And when you're done, he'll leave first. You'll hear the beep when his door shuts. If for some reason, you don't like what he's doing, just say the word 'stop' and we'll intervene."

"Got it." I already know that's not going to be an issue.

As soon as he walks out of the room and shuts the door behind him, I take off my clothes except for my lingerie. I tiptoe into the play room and slide across the silky, purple sheets on the bed and under the curtain. Lying on my back, all I can hear is the sound of my heart beating relentlessly in my ear, at least, until the door on the other side of the room opens and the sound of steps come closer. It's time.

ELEVEN

Kai

———

The first thing I see when I enter the room are pink panties. No, that's a lie. I notice her. I take a few steps into the room. My bare feet feel heavy as she comes more into my line of vision. Her legs are toned. Her calf muscles flex as she pulls her legs up and crosses her ankles. I don't know if she planned this or not, but her perfect toes match her panties ... well, perfectly. I have never been a fan of pink until now.

Much to my displeasure, her face is hidden by a purple curtain, likely the one I was behind days ago. Her body is laid out, as if this was a feast, and yet I can't look into her eyes when I make her come. That part bothers me. I want to know what she looks like. I want to feel her penetrating gaze bore into my eyes as my mouth descends onto her pussy. My hand absentmindedly runs over my bare chest. I dressed this way for her, hoping she could see what I have to offer.

My head tilts to the side as I take in the sight of her breasts, and imagine what her peaked nipples will taste like in my mouth, how her flesh will feel against the calloused parts of my hands. My desire to be with her grows the harder my dick becomes. I stand by my original assessment of this place. It's some sort of sorcery, some voodoo sex magic that turns men into beasts.

The bed sags slightly from my weight and I barely catch the intake of air this woman has inhaled. Is she nervous? I am. It's one thing to sit in a chair and get a blowjob, to pretend the woman sucking your dick is anyone from your fantasy repertoire. But to see her in the flesh, to know I can put my mouth on her, that my hands can caress her body, that my fingers can dig into her skin, knowing that she is here willingly ... this pushes any sex fantasy I have ever had out the door.

The rough exterior of my jeans presses against my growing dick, causing friction that is both welcomed and agonizing. My cock has a mind of its own right now. Truth is, it doesn't matter that I haven't seen her face; I'm attracted to her body and the fact that she trusts me.

My hand shakes as I reach out to touch her. Instinctively I pull back, afraid that she will sense that I'm nervous. I'm not, yet part of me feels that this is wrong. I have never had to pay for sex. But I'm here, paying to return the favor to this woman who gave me one of the best blowjobs I have ever had.

Everything about her seems perfect—from the curve of her hip that beckons to be held by my hand, to her supple breasts that will fit in my palm, to her strong legs that will no doubt fit over my hips. I should be so lucky to find myself in that position, where I'm centered and ready to enter her core, to bring her pleasure with my dick.

I realize in this moment that I can't do this. That being with her, in a paid situation, is not what I want. My mouth opens, intent on saying my name and giving her my phone number, but words escape me. My hand hangs in shame as I get off the bed and take a tentative step toward the door.

The sound of silk brushing against flesh has me turning around. This woman, she wants this from me. Her once closed legs are now spread wide. My knees press against the mattress as I stare at the darker pink spot of her panties. She's wet. Eager.

And I'm hungry.

She beckons me without movement or sound. Her legs drop and spread, reminding me why I'm there. She is mine for the taking. I kneel between her legs and move my hands up her limbs, kneading her muscles as I move higher until my fingers touch the lace of her underwear. I have a primal urge to rip them off, to tear them from her body as if they have offended me in some way, but I don't. I fist them tightly and place a kiss on her inner thigh.

She gasps and shakes slightly. On the inside, I'm laughing. Not at her, but at the reaction because I haven't done anything yet to equate that type of response. I will though, and I'm not going to stop until she's fucking my face and coming all over my tongue.

Now I'm a man on a mission. Determined to elicit the most glorious sounds out of this woman. I pull the wet crotch of her panties aside and inhale her sweet scent. My cock presses against my jeans, trying to break the confines of well-stitched material so he can be free. My only relief is to push harder into the mattress, trick him into thinking he's getting some action. This woman smells of lavender with a hint of vanilla and possibly cinnamon. She makes me want to devour her. She's not bare, leaving a light smattering of hair. It gives off an air of innocence, and I find that I like it. I'm so used to women being waxed that it gets old.

My nose traces along her folds, and ever so lightly I

exhale hot air into her core. Each movement causes her muscles to twitch. I love that she's nervous, that we are in the same boat. Her hips buck lightly, spurring me on.

Sitting back, I pull her panties down her legs and stuff them in my pocket for later. Without hesitation my hand swoops under her ass, and in one quick motion, my face is nestled between her legs. My tongue darts out and tastes her for the first time. She delves her fingers into my hair, her hips bucking and a whispered, "Oh, God," being said in a room where we're not allowed to talk.

And I'm smiling.

Pulling both hands out from her under her, one massages her breast, tweaking her nipple while the other parts her folds with my fingers. My mouth waters at the sight of her clit, just waiting for attention. I kiss her there, sucking her bud into my mouth and vigorously flicking it with the tip of my tongue. Her grip on my hair grows tighter, and her back arches.

I inhale her sweet scent again before trailing my tongue down her pussy. My eyes roll back in my head as I swallow her taste. *Fucking heaven.* My tongue makes its way up and down, exploring her lips and delicate folds, probing gently into her core, savoring every bit of her that I can.

My free hand switches to her other breast. I'm desperate to suck on her nipples, but my mouth is happy where it's at. As I tongue fuck her, I flick her clit with my thumb while my other hand kneads her tit. She moans, pulls my hair, and grinds her pussy against my face as if she needs me to fuck her harder.

Her hips buck wildly, and I know she's about to come. I need to feel her though and if it's not against my dick, my fingers are the best bet. Slowly, I push one in and she gasps. Her wetness coats my fingers. All I want to do is suck them off. The moans that escapes her lips are so fucking sexy it makes me harder than I've ever been before. She thrashes against the bed, rolling from side to side. My thumb presses down on her clit and she stills. Using this to my advantage, I kiss my way up her body while my finger pumps in and out of her.

She palms one of her of breasts, making me slightly jealous, but eager to watch. I take the other one in my mouth, not caring if this was part of our agreement or not. I *need* this, and want her to feel the sensation. My tongue swirls around her nipple as I add another finger inside of her. Another "Oh God," is muttered from her lips and the sharp intake of air shows me that I'm making her feel good. She wants to cry out even though she is holding back.

With my dick nestled against her hip, I rock against her, trying to find some relief before I explode. This friction is better than nothing, except I'm on the verge of coming in my jeans.

The sweet sounds coming from her mouth are too much for me to take. I'm on the brink of whipping my dick out and fucking her, but I refuse to be the man who violates her trust. I move to her other breast, sliding her hand out of the away. My teeth pull on her taut nipple while my fingers thrust in and out of her.

I move back down her body, mostly because I love the way the friction feels on my dick. The hand job I give myself in the bathroom after this is going to be epic. Hell, once I touch my dick, I'll fucking come.

With my fingers still bringing her pleasure, I turn my attention to her clit and suck it ever so softly. Her walls contract slightly, warning me that she's close. Not to leave her hanging, I speed up my hand, pushing my fingers deeper and curling them to hit her g-spot. My mouth teases her clit, nipping and sucking until her hips are springing off the mattress and she's slamming her pussy into my face.

Fucking glorious.

Resting my arm over her stomach, I pin her to the bed and continue to work her clit over with my firm tongue and the consistent strokes of my fingers. Her legs begin to quiver and her thighs start to close in around my head.

She gasps loudly and that's when I hear her fucking sinful voice. "Mmhmm ... don't stop. Please don't stop."

As if I would.

"Come for me, baby," I say without thinking.

Her hips buck wildly as she comes all over my fingers. I plant my face between her legs and taste her as if I'm starving. She continues to writhe in pleasure, her legs opening and closing against my head as I lick every last drop away from her body. I wouldn't trade this moment for anything.

Actually, I would. I'd love to see her face, to kiss her and ask her if this has been worth it for her. I'd give her my number and ask her out to dinner so I can find out what her favorite color, movie, and song is.

After several seconds, I rest my head on her thigh. Her hand returns to my hair, her fingers moving in and out in a caring fashion. I tell myself not to get attached, but I fear it may be too late.

I think about wiping my face on the sheets, but don't. I kiss every piece of her body that I can before I back my way out of the room, never taking my eyes off of her. Something inside of me tells that this is the last time. That whatever we've done here is complete. The thought of not seeing her doesn't sit well with me, but there really isn't anything I can do about that. Silently, I tell her good-bye and hope that I can meet her someday.

TWELVE

Alexandria

I've walked down the bread aisle twice and both times fail to grab my favorite creamy peanut butter. That's how preoccupied my mind has been since last night in the play room.

I can still remember the way it felt to orgasm with a man's tongue on my clit. Just thinking about it now makes me tremble. I keep thinking about what I need to do next and I come up blank. I feel like we're past the oral sex, as silly as that sounds.

I check my phone to see if I've missed a text from Jared, but there's nothing. A part of me thinks I should make the next move, but I don't want to appear desperate. I'm not a girl who has to pay for sex. Yes, I'm a virgin, but it's not because I'm ugly and can't get a date. I'm just inexperienced and men my age want someone who knows what they're doing.

Grabbing the peanut butter, I set it in my cart and head for the produce section. The girls and I were given the day off since there was nothing to do. In the catering business, it's not uncommon for there to be days when we're not busy.

The only problem is that I don't get paid when we're not working.

Once in the produce section, I reach for a package of strawberries, only for someone to try for the same one. Our hands touch and I pull back. "Sorry about that," the man says.

I recognize his voice immediately and look up at him. Standing in front of me is my high school sweetheart and the first guy I ever fell in love with. We both knew it wouldn't work when he went away to college. He looks the same as he did in high school; tall and handsome with auburn hair and green eyes. "Oh my God, is it really you?" Matt chuckles and I hug him. "It's been so long."

He hugs me tight and lets go. "That it has. How have you been?" Grabbing the strawberries, he puts them in my cart. "I didn't know you were in Portland. I figured you'd still be in Sweet Briar."

I try not to let his comment bother me. "I've been gone for a few years. Things have changed."

His smile widens. "I can see that. You're still as beautiful now as you were then."

The heat rises to my cheeks and I grin. "Thanks. You're looking good, too."

He glances down at my ring finger. "I take it you're not married."

I shake my head. "Not yet. You?"

"Same. I just finished up law school and now I'm working in Vancouver at Marshall and Vaughn Law Firm."

"That's awesome. I'm so happy for you. I'm working for a catering company until I can branch out and start my own business."

"You always wanted to be a chef," he replies warmly. "I

have to say, I sure do miss your cooking. Lunch period at school was my favorite time."

I smack his arm. "That's because you'd eat all my food. You used to drive me crazy."

We both laugh and he shakes his head. "Those were the good ole days. Sometimes I miss them. I don't see many of our friends."

"Neither do I. I pretty much work and go home." And go to Society X, but I'm not about to tell him that. Speaking of the club, I slide my hand over the top of my shirt to make sure my necklace can't be seen.

Matt pulls out his phone. "If you don't mind, I'd love to get your number. Maybe we can go out some time."

"Sure," I say without thinking. I give him my number and vice versa.

He smiles again and we hug. "I'm so glad I ran into you. I've thought a lot about you the past few years."

"Ditto," I reply in all honesty. I've often wondered where he was in life and if he was happy.

"I'll call you tonight."

He lets me go and I nod. "Okay."

Once he walks off, I'm stuck standing by the strawberries, completely at a loss for words. A part of me is ecstatic to see Matt again, but then the other half feels guilty for even considering going out with someone else. Why do I feel guilty? I don't even know the guy in the club. He's probably a player. However, hearing his last words when he left the play room makes me think otherwise.

Pulling out my phone, I call Dani. "What's up, chickadee?"

"I need your help. Can you meet me for dinner tonight?"

"Sure can. Is this about your happy time in the play room last night?"

I snort. "You have no idea. Meet me at Oscar's."

I HEAD TO OSCAR'S, which is a prime steakhouse in downtown Portland. It has the best filet in town, and it has private seating. The stuff I want to tell Dani doesn't need to be heard by anyone. Dani isn't at the restaurant when I arrive so the hostess seats me first. She has short, black hair and a kind smile. I love when restaurants have friendly staff. That's going to be requirement when I open my own place one day.

"Would you like anything to drink while you wait?" the hostess asks.

I nod. "A glass of Riesling, please."

She nods. "I'll tell your waiter."

Not long after that, the waiter stops by and sets down my glass of wine just as Dani turns the corner. She sits across from me, and smiles at our waiter who is an older gentleman with graying dark hair and tanned skin.

"May I please have a gin and tonic?"

"Of course." He nods and strolls off.

Not wasting any time, Dani scoots closer to the table. "Tell me everything. What happened last night?"

Leaning forward, I lower my voice. "He went down on me last night. It felt so damn good. I've never had anyone do that before."

Giggling, she slaps a hand over her mouth. "That's freaking hot. I seriously need to go there. Care to go with me one night?"

"Sure. I'd love to. Maybe Jared will see you and give you the tour."

Picking up her napkin, she fans herself. "Whew, I can't wait. I'm already hot just thinking about it."

The waiter comes back and gives her the gin and tonic. We order our food and I get right down to business. "What should I do next?" I ask.

Her brows furrow. "What do you mean?"

I shrug. "I don't know. Should I request another oral meeting or step it up? I know we've only met twice, but I don't think any of the foreplay stuff is going to last with us. I want more and I *know* he does."

Dani glances around to make sure no one's near before focusing back on me. "Maybe you should try the dark room. You're twenty-five years old. Surely, you weren't expecting to be a virgin until you got married, right?"

I shake my head. "No, but I didn't want to just lose it to anyone like everyone else I know."

Dani shrugs. "It's up to you, girlie. If you and this guy have a connection, it could be pretty romantic. Granted, you won't be able to see each other in the dark room, but at least, you'll get to experience being with someone fully. It'll get you prepared for someone real."

He is real. The words echo in my head, but I'm probably never going to know who he is. However, there is someone who's real in my life. "I think I have another problem," I whisper.

"What?" She takes a sip of her drink.

"I ran into someone from my past today. Do you remember Matt Davenport?"

Eyes wide, she gasps. "Are you serious? He was the love of your life."

"Exactly," I groan. "He wants to go out and I can't date him *and* participate in the club. It's not right."

With a heavy sigh, she nods. "You're right, you can't. I guess it's up to you to decide. Matt is your past, but this mystery guy could be your future. Do you want safe or sexy and adventurous with risk?"

I guzzle down the rest of my wine, my stomach in knots. I know what my body wants, but my head is screaming at me to turn to Matt.

"I don't know," I murmur, "but I'll figure it out."

After we finish eating, I head home and turn on my laptop. Dani's question should be simple to answer. Do I want safe or sexy and adventurous with risk? A part of me wants safe just so I know I won't get hurt, but then the other part wants to take the risk, even if I get hurt.

Matt is a sweet guy, but I don't see him being able to quench my desires. It's crazy because in high school, those kinds of things didn't matter to me. However, I did love him deeply. Even now, there's still a part of me that wonders what would've happened if I allowed our relationship to grow instead of letting him go, knowing he would have sex in college.

Grabbing a bottle of wine out of the refrigerator, I open it up and drink straight from it. I check my emails and catch up on everyone's posts on Facebook. I drink more of my wine until I realize almost half the bottle is gone. My body feels weightless and I love the feeling. I can't stop thinking about my night in the play room. There's something about being in the club that turns me on. It must be the lack of inhibitions. It's like anything I do there is acceptable, not like in our society. Back in my hometown, I'd be viewed as a whore.

"Fuck it," I mutter, slurring the words.

I type in *passionate sex* in the search engine and hit *Go*. I've watched all sorts of porno movies about blowjobs but never ones about people actually having sex. A ton of videos pop up and I click on a random one, praying like hell a virus doesn't get put on my laptop. The movie starts and the couple is on a bed, fully clothed and kissing. It's very sensual. The guy unbuttons her shirt and sucks her breasts. My nipples tingle just watching it. Ever so slowly, their clothes come off and he enters her. For the next thirty minutes, my eyes are glued to the screen, watching them have sex in multiple positions. It's so erotically hot it makes everything inside of me tighten. I'm one step closer to the final decision.

THIRTEEN

Kai

———

I need a friend. A best friend, guy friend, bro, or whatever else they're called so I can unload about my life.

Turmoil. It's what I feel. Last night I thought of a hundred different ways I could find out this woman's name, only to picture myself behind bars for breaking the law. A law that likely doesn't exist, but because that club is nothing but voodoo magic I'd probably end up in a dungeon somewhere, and no one would know where I am.

Sitting beside me is Bryant. He's rambling on about someone he met last night who happens to be normal. His description not mine. I'm going out on a limb here and am going to say that the woman he met isn't an employee of Society X. Not that there is anything wrong with women or men working there.

I've thought about telling Bryant about my two visits, but can't stomach his reaction, mostly because I've been with the same woman and he's boasted that members have their pick. Thing is, I never wanted to sign up to begin with, but now that I have, I don't know if I can stop.

I tell myself that if Jenica were to text me with a new offer, I'd tell her no. But the thought of completely anonymous foreplay or sex is exciting. It's fucking exhilarating. After I jacked off last night, I felt like I was walking on cloud nine. I know I pleasured her. I was there when she came all over my fingers. The best part is, I learned more about myself as a lover. I learned to watch her body for signs and perform to what she desired. She didn't have to tell me anything, except she did.

I'll never forget her gasping loudly as she was about to come or her raspy voice telling me not to stop. Nor will I ever forget my major flub of calling her baby. Never have I been a man to give pet nicknames to women, but last night when the words slipped out of my mouth they felt right. All of this feels right, except for the fact that I don't know what she looks like or her name.

Bryant continues to talk about his girlfriend, or soon-to-be one, while I navigate us toward Sweet Briar. He's working with me today to develop our marketing campaign. Parker says he's the best, and while I have no reason not to believe my boss, Bryant comes off as flakey. I really need someone who knows what they're doing so this revitalization project goes off without a hitch. Not only do we have to bring big business to town, we need to make sure there are people here to sustain the economy. Sweet Briar needs to become the place to be.

As I pull into the church, the resident preacher is standing on the steps. Larry waves. "Good morning, Mr. Robicheau."

"Please, call me Kai," I say as I greet him on the steps. Bryant is right behind me and introductions are made. Stan Meyer, the man who claims to be mayor of this fading town, steps out of the church. He seems happy, and for the life of me I can't fathom why. If I attached my name to the title of Mayor I'd do anything I could to make my town successful. And with Sweet Briar being on the coast, the ideas are endless.

I shake hands with Stan, out of professional courtesy, but there's something about him that rubs me the wrong way. There isn't a doubt in my mind that once Sweet Briar is looking like it's old self again that he doesn't take credit for spearheading the project.

"I brought plans," I tell the men as I hold up a large roll of designs. I follow them into the church where a long table is set up.

"Will this do?" Larry asks.

"It's perfect. Let me show you what I have." Removing the rubber band, I let the papers roll somewhat flat. "You've already seen the design for the housing complex, but I wanted you to see what we have in mind for the shopping center."

I give Larry and Stan a chance to look over what I've come up with. "As you can see, I've gone retro with the design. After sifting through old town records, I found a bylaw that states all buildings must conform to the listed specifications. Unfortunately, in each update of the law, that requirement hasn't changed, which necessarily isn't a problem, except for the previous builders didn't follow code.

"I spent some time at the library, searching for pictures of Sweet Briar to aid in my design. So what you're seeing here is the seventies version of what construction looked like and what is allowed by the bylaw."

"But this is a new generation," Stan says.

I nod. "It is. However, you have to look at the generation that will be coming here to visit. They'll appreciate seeing buildings that remind them of their childhood. We're going to bring back those memories," I say as I flip a few pages into my design. "Ward Enterprises recently acquired this building. With its beachfront access, we're going to give it an open concept and turn it into an arcade. One that serves children, teens, and adults."

"Our focus is to draw tourism," Bryant states. "By creating a place that not only reminds adults of the place where they met their first love, or the summer they spent watching the sunrise with their friends, but where they can bring their families."

"We're creating nostalgia," I add. My eyes are focused on Larry, not so much Stan, although when I do look at him, he seems confused. Personally, I don't think it's a hard concept to follow. Retro is all the rage right now, and with a small town like Sweet Briar, people will talk about how welcoming it was while they were here.

"Do you have any questions?"

Rubbing his face, Stan nods. "I guess I don't get it."

"What part?" Bryant asks.

"Why wouldn't we build industrial?"

Bryant and I both laugh, except it's not a "ha-ha you're funny" but a "you've got to be kidding me" type.

"Industrial screams, 'pass through our town because we have nothing to offer.' That is the last thing we want. We want people to pass through and stop. We want them to find a place they fall in love with so that they come back. Ward Enterprises is here to make that happen, Stan. We're investing millions into recreating this town so that people want to live here, work here, and visit. Industrial isn't welcoming."

"Well as Mayor—"

"Unelected," Larry points out. I want to laugh but know it'd be unprofessional.

That seems to put Stan in his place. "I like what I'm seeing and I agree, my childhood had some of the best memories. And you're right, I moved here with my family because of it. I will admit, though, the idea makes me nervous."

"We'll do a market analysis," Bryant says. "We can still start building. It won't slow us down at all."

"That is the best idea you've had all morning," Stan adds. I glance quickly at Bryant who is clenching his jaw. The analysis is to appease Larry, not prove that we're wrong because we're not. We know this business inside and out.

"Let's grab some lunch, shall we?" Larry asks, trying to diffuse the growing situation. Stan needs to be reminded that he had nothing to do with Ward Enterprises getting involved. It was all Parker and Pastor Larry.

We follow Larry through the church, down the back stairs, and into a small meeting area. There are a few older women, scurrying around to make sure the meal they've prepared is ready to go. My stomach growls at the smell of gravy and roast.

"I hope you're hungry," Larry says with a smile. He has no idea how hungry I am right now. Bryant and I follow Larry to a table and sit down. Our food is placed on the table in home-style fashion, yet another nod to my retro building idea. Bryant elbows me to make sure I recognize that we're on the same page.

"So, Kai, tell me about yourself," Larry asks as he plops a heap of potatoes onto his plate. My mouth waters, waiting for my turn.

"Well, I was born in Arizona, obtained my degree in Urban Development. Took a job with the company I interned with before transferring to Utah for a year to work on a redevelopment project. That job led to Malibu, California, which is where Parker Ward found me. He wooed me for a few months until I finally caved and moved to Portland to work on the Sweet Briar project."

"Are you married? Kids?" he asks.

I shake my head. "Single. No kids."

"That he's aware of," Bryant the douchebag says.

I glare at him, letting him know I don't appreciate the inappropriate comment.

An arm reaches in between Larry and I, and I smile at the woman who fills my water glass. "Thank you."

"Sounds like he's about perfect for Lexi," she says.

"Oh, Lois," Larry says.

"What? Our Lexi is gorgeous and deserves a good man. She's living up in that city all by herself and Kai here is new. I bet she could show him around."

"I'm sorry, who is Lexi?" I ask.

"My daughter," Larry sighs, yet he's smiling. I can't tell if he's upset with her or proud of her.

"She's single," Lois says before heading back to the other women. I watch her closely and can tell that she's talking about me. The women giggle, causing me to blush.

"Lexi has a good heart, so if you're looking for someone to show you around, she'd gladly do it. She recently finished school and is a chef. Boy, my daughter can sure cook."

"Food is the way to a man's heart," Bryant adds.

"Let me give you her number just in case you find yourself bored some day and want to go site-seeing." Larry writes her number down on a piece of paper. I take it and read it over, but something doesn't feel right. I know I'm not in a relationship, but it feels like one. A very odd one to boot, but I'd be afraid of getting involved with Lexi and her finding out about my escapades at Society X.

Of course, thinking about the club and the things that

have happened in there have me thinking about the mysterious woman and whether I'll get a chance to see her again. I want to, but I'm not sure in what capacity. The play room is supposed to be about fetishes, I'm not sure how I'd react if she summoned me to suck on her toes. A spanking, I could probably do. I've always wanted to play with a flogger, but have never had the chance. I would draw the line at putting on a diaper though. Pretending I'm a baby doesn't turn me on, and if there's one thing that I'm adamant about, it's making sure my partner and I are both satisfied.

Setting her number down on the table, I turn my attention to my lunch. This home-cooked meal is a Godsend. I can't cook for shit, and this is the best meal I've had in a long time.

When we're done, I notice the piece of paper is gone. I could say something, but I don't want Larry to think that I'm interested or that I might call. The last thing I want is for him to tell his daughter to expect a phone call from me and it never happens. Clearly, the sorcery of Society X is working against me right now, which makes me what to reach out to Jenica. Although, I don't know what I'd say.

FOURTEEN

Alexandria

I spent the past couple of days thinking about nothing but the pros and cons of doing the unthinkable. What kind of person goes to a sex club to lose their virginity? Me, that's who. There's seriously something wrong with me. A part of me wonders if it's because I've been such a good girl my whole life, and now, the wild side of me has the freedom to do whatever it wants. Either way, I've made my choice. Or at least, I think I have.

The traffic is horrible this morning as I head toward the shop. Adrenaline courses through my veins, and I know it's now or never. When I come to a stop at one of the traffic lights, I pull out my phone. Jared's name is programmed into it so I press the call button. He picks up on the second ring.

"Good morning, Alexandria. What can I do for you this morning?"

I suck in a breath and speak quickly, "I want an appointment in the dark room."

"I'm sure I can get that scheduled. Is there a specific time or date you have in mind?" he asks.

"As soon as possible. Preferably tonight." I want to do it now while I have the courage.

"Okay, I'll see what I can do. Do you want me to pair you with a partner or do you prefer the same one you've had?"

"Same one. I don't want anyone else."

"We'll contact him right away. I'll call you as soon as I have an answer."

"Sounds good." My hands shake as I hang up the phone. I'm so nervous, and yet, terrified to hear the verdict. If he turns me down, I'll never go back to Society X again. Maybe I'm stupid for even going in the first place, but I keep getting drawn back.

I arrive at the Let's Get Baked shop and Adrienne is already inside with Sandy. "Good morning," I announce, walking through the door.

Sandy waves. "Good morning, sweet pea. We got a busy day today. Brenda from the real estate office called me last night and said she wanted fried chicken instead of baked for her employees." She shrugs. "Apparently, that's what they all want. I need you to make your famous macaroni and cheese. It was requested."

"What does Alex make that isn't famous?" Adrienne says with a laugh.

I smack her blonde ponytail in passing. She has two packs of strawberries in front of her and I know exactly what she's going to bake. "What about your strawberry cake? It's been in tons of magazines."

She brushes off her shoulders and winks. "It has, hasn't it?"

The smell of the fryers come to life, and Sandy's already putting in the flour coated chicken. My stomach growls; I'll have to make sure I steal a couple of pieces before we take it over to our clients. Grabbing the macaroni out of the pantry, I fix two pots of boiling water and toss the noodles inside.

Out of breath, Dani charges through the door. "Sorry, I'm late. There was a wreck I got stuck behind. I thought I'd never get here."

Sandy waves her off. "We're good on time. Just get started on the green beans and sweet carrots. The ladies at the real estate office want a country meal and that's exactly what we're going to give them."

"They need to visit North Carolina Mountains," Adrienne replies. "There's this place I visited with my husband that has the best southern comfort food."

Lips pursed, Dani places her hands on her hips. "Are you saying it's better than what we can do?"

Adrienne throws a strawberry at her, and Dani catches and eats it with a smug smile. "Of course not," Adrienne laughs. "I'm just saying it was really good. Hearing the accents over there is pretty interesting."

"I've never been farther east than Wyoming." Just saying that proves I didn't travel much as a child. While my friends traveled the world with their families, I was stuck in Sweet Briar. My trip to Wyoming was with some of my friends in college.

Dani walks over to Adrienne and me, her voice low as she looks at me. "Want to go to Society X tonight?"

Adrienne shakes her head, her focus on the strawberries. "You two are so bad."

I move closer to Dani. "I might have a date in the dark room."

Both of their eyes widen and they gasp. "Seriously?" Dani squeals. "You decided to do it?"

"Yeah, if I don't back out. I'm so nervous." My macaroni noodles are done, so I drain the water out of the pots and set them aside. Dani and Adrienne's eyes are focused solely on me. My cheeks burn and I know they're bright red.

"Are you sure this is what you want?" Adrienne asks. "You can't take back your virginity once you lose it."

I shrug. "I'm going to lose it eventually, right? I've been with the same man the past two times in the play room. I might not know who he is, but I have a connection with him I haven't had with anyone else."

Dani agrees with a nod and looks at Adrienne. "She speaks the truth. I've heard the stories. You should've been here to hear them." Then she turns back to me. "With it being your first time, it's going to hurt at first. Does this guy know you're a virgin?"

I close my eyes. "No."

Both Dani and Adrienne sigh. Adrienne touches my elbow and I open my eyes. "Don't you think he deserves to know? Taking a woman's virginity is a big deal."

"I know," I whisper. "I'll find a way to tell him." I walk away to grab the shredder, hoping like hell they'll want to talk about something else when I return. When I join them again, Dani opens her mouth to speak, but I turn to Adrienne. "How are you doing anyway? We heard you were sick."

Adrienne rubs her belly. "I had a stomach bug. The baby and I are okay. I had to make sure to drink lots of fluids. The doctor said I was going to need an IV if I didn't start keeping things down."

Placing my hand on her shoulder, I squeeze it gently. "We're glad you're okay. I'm going to miss you when you go on maternity leave."

She snorts. "Me too. I'm already missing out on the juicy stories."

Dani winks at her. "Don't worry. I'm sure Alex will fill you in on the dirty details."

Rolling my eyes, I laugh and walk away. Before I can open the refrigerator doors, my phone vibrates in my pocket. I pull it out and my heart begins to race. Sandy isn't paying attention to me so I sneak off inside the pantry.

I accept the call, making sure to keep my voice around a whisper. "Hello," I answer.

"Alexandria, it's Jared. I have some good news."

My pulse spikes even more. "You do?"

"Mm-hmm. Your partner has agreed to meet you in the dark room. The only available time we have is nine o'clock. Does that work for you?"

"Yes," I blurt. "I can do that."

"Great. I have you down. See you tonight."

"See ya." I hang up the phone and close my eyes. I'm going to lose my virginity tonight.

BEFORE GOING TO THE CLUB, I go home, take a shower, and change clothes. My hair smelled like fried chicken, which is not exactly the scent I want to smell like. Jared meets me at the front and we go through the security process like usual. Once we're in the back hallway, I count down the seconds before I enter the dark room. Jared opens the door to what will be my dressing room and then he opens the black door across the room. It's pitch black inside, but the light helps me to see a little.

"When you're ready, just go through this door and make your way to the bed. Your partner will be in momentarily afterwards. When you get done, just come over to your door and press the button. The door will open and you'll be let inside without your partner seeing you."

I nod in understanding. "Got it."

He nods once and starts for the door. "Have fun."

My heart's pounding so hard I can feel it in my throat. Even my teeth are chattering. Tonight, I didn't even bother with lingerie. No one was going to see it. With shaking hands, I take off my clothes and sneak into the dark room, using the wall as a guide toward the bed. The sheets are silky against my back as I lie down on them. I keep hoping my eyes will adjust to the darkness, but I can't see a damn thing.

The sound of a door opens and I hold my breath. Biting my lip, I grip a handful of the sheets in my fists. I can hear his breathing as he approaches, all deep and full of anticipation. The bed dips down and a hand slides up my leg and stops at my thigh. His other hand touches my shoulder and moves up my neck. The warmth of his body seeps into mine. The next thing I know, his lips are on mine, his tongue gently finding his way inside of me. I want to talk to him, but I'm so nervous. His legs tangle with mine and I can feel how hard he is for me. Everything inside of me clenches. All I can feel is his mouth on me, sucking my nipples and touching me like he's a starved man. His groans are enough to drive me over the edge. He kisses my stomach on down to between my legs and licks my clit once, making me gasp at the contact. A deep chuckle escapes his lips as he spreads my legs wide.

I hear the sound of a wrapper opening, and I'm pretty sure it's him putting on a condom. As he moves closer, I can feel the tip of him at my opening. My breaths come out faster. "Wait," I whisper, placing my hands on his shoulders.

"Are you okay?" he whispers back.

I slide my hands up his shoulders to his face. It's the first time I've been able to feel what he looks like. His face is smooth and he has soft hair I can run my hands through. It makes me wonder what color his hair and eyes are.

"There's something you should know."

"What is it?" He sounds concerned and I like it.

"I'm a virgin." I can hear the intake of his breath. Everything after that comes to a halt and I hold my breath. I can still feel the tip of him at my core, still hard and ready to go. "I understand if you don't want to go through with it."

He places a finger on my lips. "I'm just shocked. I'll go slowly. I promise."

His lips press to mine, very gentle and warm. The next thing I know, his hand is between my legs, his fingers fondling my clit. I open my legs wider and he slips one inside. Arching my back, I give into his touch, moaning in delight as he explores me with his fingers. All too soon, he pulls them out, leaving me breathless.

Using his tongue, he licks a path all the way up my leg to the inside of my thigh before sucking on the spot that ached to feel his touch again. Nuzzling my clit with his nose, he enters me with his tongue. I grab his hair and moan, so close to losing control. Chuckling, he moves away, continuing his torturous path up my body to my breasts.

"That's not funny," I whisper.

He bites one of my nipples and I gasp. "Your orgasms tonight will be with me inside of you."

As he wraps his warm lips around my nipple, my whole body tightens with need. Pressing his hips against mine, he positions himself between my legs, grazing his cock along my opening.

"Are you ready?" he murmurs.

I nod even though he can't see me. "Yes."

Taking my face in his hands, he lowers his lips to mine and stays there, breathing me in with just the gentlest of touches. When he pulls back, he caresses my cheeks with his thumbs and tenderly pushes inside of me until he's all the way in.

I bite my lip to keep from crying out. It hurts, but it's a good sort of pain.

"I'll stop if I'm hurting you." He carefully thrusts his hips.

"You're good," I breathe. "Keep going."

He moves slowly, our hips pushing against each other. It's almost like he's making love to me, but I know that's not what this is. I can always pretend. What's crazy is I can feel the connection all the way down to my soul.

Pressing his lips to mine, he caresses my tongue, his thrusts deep and slow. His torturous pace only heightens my desire. I lock my legs around his waist and hold on while moving my hips against his.

Picking up his pace, he moans. "Let it go, baby, so I can come inside of you."

His words are all it takes to send me over the edge. Gripping his shoulders, my skin tingles and my toes curl as the longest and strongest orgasm I've ever felt explodes across my entire body. His body jerks and I can feel his cock pulsating as his release overtakes him. Even though I'm a little sore, I feel like I'm on cloud nine. He slides out of me and holds my face in his hands as he kisses me. I place my hands over his and squeeze.

"Goodnight."

It's all I can say before I'm heading for the door and hurrying out of the dark room.

FIFTEEN

Kai

The doom and gloom of the weather matches my outlook on life right now. Ever since my night in the dark room, I have been despondent. I've been going through the motions on automatic pilot because I'm unable to fully grasp what the fuck took place. She's a virgin ... or was until I took that sacred piece from her. For the second time, I almost got up and left her there, but something told me to stay, to give her what she wanted.

And I did. I took her virginity when it should've been given to someone who cares about her, who loves her unconditionally, who fucking deserved it because that man is not me. Any man who has to pay for sex doesn't deserve the virtue of another, and yet I took it like a greedy motherfucker because I felt sorry for her.

Every time I think about those whispered words, my heart breaks. Any man would've high-tailed it out of that room, but not me. I couldn't. As much as my mind wanted to, my heart told me to give her what she was asking for. When she flew off the bed, I stayed there, trying to come to terms with what just happened. Why did this woman need to seek this sort of attention at a sex club? Is there something wrong with her? Has society shunned her in some way?

As far as I'm concerned, I'm done with the club. I thought about blocking Jenica's number from my phone, but truthfully, if she were to text, I'd answer. I'm determined to break the rules. To rip the shroud covering our faces away so we can see each other. So we can look into each other's eyes, smile, and appreciate the pleasure that we're giving one another. No more secrecy. It makes me feel like I'm using this woman, and I'm not.

Standing in front of my living room window, I gaze down at the street, trying to make heads or tails of everything that is going on in my mind. It's been raining for days, which is perfect for the mood I've been in.

Except tonight I must put on a suit, a fucking bright ass smile, and charm the pants off investors. Parker Ward is hosting a dinner at his house and I'm expected to be there when it's the last place I want to be.

However, anything I can do to get my mind off the fuckery of this week, I'll do it. To put my man card back in my wallet and forget that I took some stranger's virginity. I don't care if I had intimate knowledge of her beforehand, I can't get this shit out of my head.

The rain covers my window faster than my wipers can move it away. I officially hate Portland and everything it stands for. I plan to tell Parker that Sweet Briar is going to be my only project, except I don't know how to tell him the reason why. It's not like I can say, "Hey, I fucked some chick in this sex club and now I want to get the fuck out of town." He'd probably fire me on the spot for being some sexual deviant. Cut me loose before I slip up or someone sees me going in and out of there. No one wants a scandal.

I pull into the driveway of his house ... strike that,

mansion ... or is a castle? From my car I can't be sure, but it looks like the only thing missing is a moat. However, with the amount of rainfall we're getting, it won't take long for a trench to develop.

My car door is opened and an umbrella is promptly put over my head so I can step out. "Mr. Robicheau, welcome to Ward Manor," the valet says. I have hob knobbed with some very famous people, but I have never been treated like this upon arrival. I'm tempted to call him Jeeves, but don't want to insult him.

"Thank you." I reach for the umbrella, but he motions for me to walk toward the house. He stays in line with me until I reach the front door where the doorman greets me. He shows me into the vast foray with its grand chandelier hanging overhead and the wide staircase that has a banister that any teen would want to slide down. I'm starting to think Parker's married to a princess or something equally defining because this house is fit for royalty.

"The party is through those doors," the doorman says, pointing to my left. I nod, acting as casual as I can, pretending that I knew that and I wasn't just standing in awe of the most gorgeous room I have ever been in.

I walk through the double doors into the ballroom. People are mingling around the circular tables that have been set up while caterers walk around with trays of hors d'oeuvres and champagne. I snag a crab cake and flute filled with bubbly before making my way toward Parker.

There's a blonde-haired woman with her hand resting on Parker's arm who has to be his wife. I haven't had the pleasure of meeting her yet, but Bryant says she's a knock out. I peruse the room to see if anyone else fits the bill and my eyes land on another woman with brunette hair, but with blonde strands. Or is it the other way around? Is she a blonde with brunette? I know for a fact she can't be Parker's wife because she's dressed in a white shirt with black pants and her long hair is pulled into a low ponytail. Not to mention, she's standing behind one of the buffet tables.

"Kai, so happy you could make it." Parker's voice forces me to tear my eyes away from the caterer. I smile at him and his wife before taking her hand and pressing my lips to it. "This must be your daughter," I say jokingly, except I'm not because I wouldn't mind getting to know her a little better. Parker is one lucky son of a bitch, but I guess when you have money, you have only the finer things in life.

"Oh, I like him, Parker," she says with a cute laugh.

"This is my wife, Mia."

"It's my pleasure, ma'am."

"Please, call me Mia. Parker has told me so much about you. He also shared your plans and I have to say that I love everything you're doing. I just love Sweet Briar and can't wait to spend summers there."

Right, of course they'll have a summer home. I mean, why wouldn't they when they live in a freaking mansion?

"I really hope that once we're done, it's the place that everyone wants to be," I tell them both. Parker nods in agreement, but is unable to add his two cents because he's being pulled away, and when he leaves, his wife does, too.

I watch them for a few minutes and imagine myself as Parker with Mia or someone like Mia on my arm. They mingle and greet everyone who enters the room. Parker's head is constantly tilted toward his wife's, even more so when she speaks. It's almost as if he's hearing her voice for the first time. If that isn't love, I don't know what is.

Another tray is brought by, this time with bite-size quiches. They've never been my favorite, but I'm starving. In my recent "woe is me party," I've not eaten much.

Honestly, I've had a hard time stomaching much of anything since the move, but that's been compounded by everything else.

I have to say this quiche is satisfying, and when the tray is brought by again, I grab the last one off of it and quickly devour it. I know I'm supposed to walk around and introduce myself, but my mind is not on the job right now. I'm having a self-induced pity party over something I have no control over, and that fucking sucks.

"It was her choice," I mutter to myself.

"Bad break-up?" A hand falls hard onto my shoulder. I look to see Bryant standing next to me.

"Where's your girlfriend?"

"Couldn't make it." He doesn't seem put off by this, especially as he's surveying the room. Bryant comes off as the guy who makes shit up to impress his friends. For all I know his mystery girlfriend is an inflatable doll or one of those expensive human-like dolls that you get from Japan. I shouldn't judge him, but I can't help it.

"That's too bad. I was looking forward to meeting her."

"Let's do dinner next week," he suggests.

I nod, acting as if I'm game, wondering if that gives him time to pay someone to be his date. Man, I'm a horrible friend.

"Have her bring a friend," I say.

He chuckles hard. "Now we're talking."

Bryant starts introducing me to people. The man I know and the one standing next to me are two different people. It's like he has a shut off switch that allows him to go from crude to professional in a flash. Like I've said though, Bryant is damn good at his job otherwise I can't imagine Parker keeping him around.

Every time I move about the room, I glance back at the

buffet table to check out the beautiful woman I spotted earlier. There are a few times when I think she's staring at me, and she may have even blushed. I'm definitely gawking, taking her in. She's gorgeous, and the closer I get to her table I realize that her physical features are everything that I look for in a woman.

When we're finally told that the food is ready, I rush to try to be the first in line.

"Why does Parker have a buffet?" I ask. "I would think a served plate would be more his style."

"It is, but not Mia's. She's very humble, and so each party there's a mix of him and her. She keeps him grounded even though she's some famous designer."

"Really?"

Bryant nods as he reaches for a plate. "Yeah. A while back, Parker bought this clothing company, complete with stores, and instead of dismantling and selling it off, he brought her in to rebuild. She completely turned the company around, and within six months cleared a massive profit."

"Wow."

"Yeah, but it doesn't go to her head. She still packs Parker a paper bag lunch on the days he doesn't have any client meetings."

I stifle a laugh. It's cute though, to show your spouse that kind of love. Bryant and I move down the line, and as I get to the brunette with blonde highlights, I can't help but make eye contact with her. She stands back, with her hands clasped together, watching and waiting to see if anyone needs assistance or if a platter needs to be replaced.

"Hi," I say, loud enough that she can hear me.

She grins and shyly turns her head away. I can't tell if

she's trying to hide her reaction from me, but all it does is make me press on.

"Did you make this?" I ask, pointing to some pasta creation.

"I did," she says. Her voice hits me like a ton of bricks. It's familiar, and yet I can't place it.

"What's your name?"

"Dria," she says. I rack my brain, mentally going through my contacts. I can't recall a time, either here or in California, where I've met a Dria.

"Your voice seems familiar. You wouldn't happen to be from California?"

She shakes her head, but smiles as well. "No, sorry. Born and raised here."

The arm of the man behind me, reaches over me to scoop some pasta. That's my cue to move on, except I want to stay and chat with her. I follow Bryant to our table and make sure I choose a seat that gives me direct line of sight to where Dria stands.

"She's hot," he says, stuffing his mouth.

"Beautiful," I counter.

"You should ask her out."

Maybe I should. And the more I think about it, I want to, but it feels like I'm cheating on the mystery woman by doing that. I'm tempted to ask Bryant if he's been in any of the rooms and if so, did he feel that way, but I don't want to explain myself. It's really none of his business with what I've done in there.

As the night continues, I'm never far from the buffet table. I make sure to mingle near her, catching her eye every so often. I even toss in a wink or two for good measure. Her co-workers quickly catch on though, and from what I can tell are encouraging her to talk to me.

I'd like that. Actually, I'd love for her to ask me my name or for my number. When the caterers start to pack up, panic sets in. It's a now or nothing type moment because I don't want to go to my boss and ask him about the company he used. I will if I have to, but there are easier ways.

Excusing myself, I rush outside to find Dria loading a truck. "Excuse me," I say through the darkness, hoping not to scare her.

"Hi," she says, and once again it feels like I know her.

"My name's Kai. I'm new in town. I'm single. No children. And I'd really like to take you out for coffee or something?"

There's giggling coming from the side door. She glances over her shoulder and starts laughing. Instantly I feel like a fool. That is until she turns around and hands me a card. "Here's my number."

I take her card and stare at her perfect cursive handwriting, and when I look up, she's gone and the side door is closed. This could turn into a cat and mouse game if I rush back inside, but I'm happy with just having her number. First thing tomorrow, I'm calling her just so I can hear her voice again.

SIXTEEN

Alexandria

I have so much going on in my mind, I can't think straight. Smiling like everything's perfect is the only way I can get through it.

I feel like an idiot. Why the hell did I give that guy my number? Oh yeah, I know why ... Dani and Adrienne gave me so much hell about it that I had to. It's not like he's going to call anyway. It'll probably be better if he doesn't. I just lost my virginity in a fucking sex club to a man I don't know. How will I ever explain that to someone if I ever do get involved in a relationship?

Grabbing my T-shirt and shorts out of my closet, I slip them on and hurry back into my bathroom to dry my hair. I have thirty minutes before I have to be at work, and if I don't get out in the next five minutes, traffic will be a bitch. Luckily, I only have to work half a day so I plan on spending the rest of my afternoon at Looking Glass Falls and hiking along the trails. I need some peace and quiet.

My phone rings just as I walk out the front door. Glancing down at the screen, I smile. "Hi, Mom. Everything okay?"

She sighs. "Getting a little antsy having to stay home. I really can't wait to get back to work."

I laugh. "I bet. How's your foot?"

"Much better. The doctor says it's healing nicely. I miss going on my walks at lunchtime though. It looks like it'll be a while before I can do any long-distance walking."

Getting in my car, I head toward the shop. "You'll get back to it eventually."

"I know," she says. "Are you driving to work right now?"

"Yep. I just have half a day and then I'm going to Moulton Falls for a bit. Do you need me for something?"

"No, I'm fine, sweetheart. I was actually calling to see how the party went last night. I heard Let's Get Baked catered the food. Denise said she saw you there."

Denise is their neighbor and I do remember seeing her. She didn't recognize me until I told her who I was. "I saw her, too. She didn't know who I was."

My mother giggles. "That's what she said. She also complimented on how beautiful you were, and that city life suited you."

It was my turn to laugh. "Yeah, she made a comment on how she thought I'd be married by now with kids. Guess I fooled her."

"Yes, you did. Either way, I'm happy for you."

"That makes one of you," I mumble to myself. "All right, Mom, I'm at work. I'll call you later."

"All right, honey. I love you."

"Love you, too." Hanging up, I rest my forehead on the steering wheel. I'm sure a lot of people back home thought I'd have gotten married and became a housewife by now. I love proving people wrong.

Before I can get out of the car, my phone beeps. I hop

out and look at the screen, shocked beyond belief to see who it is.

Good morning, this is Kai. It was nice meeting you last night. I was wondering if today would be good for you to show me around?

I start to text back, but I can't seem to get my fingers to work. Instead, I hurry inside. Sandy is in her office, typing away on her computer, and she doesn't even look up when I run to Dani.

"Hey," I say, catching her off guard. Dani squeals and chocolate morsels go flying.

"Oh my God, you scared me." She holds a hand over her heart. "What's going on?"

She mixes the morsels into her cookie dough and sets the bowl in the refrigerator. I hold out my phone so she can see the text from Kai. "He texted this morning. What do I say? I wasn't expecting him to actually call."

She scoffs. "Seriously? The man couldn't stop staring at you last night." Like that makes me feel better. He could be a serial killer or a rapist.

Granted, Kai is very sexy and probably worth a million dollars by the looks of him. Why he's interested in me, I have no clue. I don't have the expensive clothes and jewelry, and I'm definitely not famous like his friend, Parker Ward.

"What do I do? I don't know the guy at all."

"Take a picture of his license and send it to me. That way, if he tries something funny, I can nail his ass."

I stare at her like she's lost her mind. "Seriously? You want me to ask for his license."

She giggles. "Why not? He'll understand. Plus, I can Google him. Maybe he just wants someone to show him around like he asked. Doesn't hurt to at least be friends. Not to mention, he's super hot and possibly loaded."

I roll my eyes. "I don't care about that. I just don't know why he picked me out. There were a ton of beautiful women there."

Adrienne squeezes my shoulders from behind. "It's because you're amazing and he can see it. Don't underestimate yourself, Alex. Just because you don't make over a million a year doesn't mean you're not worth it."

Catering to the elite has definitely given me insight on how a lot of rich people are. Some of them were friendly to me, but others, stuck their noses up like I was nothing. I know my value and I'm happy with what I've achieved in life. It's not like it would work anyway with Kai. It's clear to see we come from different worlds.

Taking a deep breath, I pull out my phone. "You're right. There's no harm in showing him around Portland."

Dani's grin widens. "Exactly."

Today sounds great. I get off around noon and then I have the rest of the day off. You can meet me at my house around 12:45.

I text him my address and his reply comes fast.

Perfect. I'll see you then.

Heart racing, I go back inside and start on my triple chocolate brownies. A part of me feels guilty, like I'm betraying the man from Society X. Then again, I'm the idiot who chose to lose her virginity to a stranger. It's embarrassing, and I'm almost thankful I don't know who the man is. It's probably best I don't go back.

I GET home in time to check my hair and makeup before the doorbell rings. Glancing out the window, I have no doubt it's Kai ... especially since there's a shiny, expensive car in the driveway. When I open the door, he takes off his sunglasses and smiles.

"Hey. Thanks for agreeing to show me around."

I can't stop my eyes from taking him all in. He looks different from the night before. Instead of wearing a nice suit, he's dressed in a pair of khaki shorts and a blue T-shirt that matches his eyes. His blondish-brown hair isn't gelled, making it look much lighter in the sun.

"Hi," I say back. "You're welcome. Happy to help."

He nods toward the cars. "Want me to drive?"

Shaking my head, I shut the door behind me. "I will. That way I can show you everything. But first, I need to take a picture of your license."

He chuckles and pulls out his wallet. "Why?"

When he hands it to me, I finally get a look at his full name. Kai Robicheau. It's an interesting last name. I clear my throat and take a picture of it. "I have to make sure you're not a serial killer." I send the picture to Dani. "You can never be too careful." I try to hide my smile and fail.

"What about you? Maybe I should see *your* license. I'm starting to think Dria might not be your real name."

I meet his blue stare. "It's close enough."

His smile widens. "Okay, I trust you. Are you ready to go?"

I nod toward my silver, Toyota Camry. "The doors are unlocked." Instead of going over to the passenger's side, he opens my door first. "Thanks," I say, heat rising to my cheeks as I get in. He then walks to the passenger's side door and opens it, the scent of his cologne drifting past my nose. It smells familiar and it makes my chest tighten. "Where do you want me to take you?" I ask.

He shrugs. "Anywhere you want."

Judging by the twinkle in his eyes, I have a feeling it's not why he asked me out. "You don't want me to show you around, do you?"

"Oh, yeah, I do. I just mainly wanted to spend time with you."

I snort. "I'm sure you could've asked anyone to do that."

"True, but I wanted you. You remind me of someone. I just can't place it."

"I doubt it. No offense, but you and I don't exactly run in the same circles." We get on the highway and I head right into downtown.

His eyes narrow. "Why do you say that?"

"Your car is more expensive than my house, Kai."

"So. That doesn't mean a thing."

We're going to see about that. I drive by a hole in the wall Italian restaurant and point at it. "Have you ever eaten in there?"

Kai looks over at it and shakes his head. I thought I'd see disgust on his face, but he genuinely seems interested. "They have the best lasagna in town. It's not the kind of place I see people like you in."

His lips pull back. "Maybe we can go there together. I'd be happy to try it out."

"Really?"

"Why not? I trust your judgment. Your food last night

was amazing. I have no doubt you know what's good and what isn't."

"Thanks. I take food seriously."

We drive down more downtown streets and I point out all my favorite spots, including the best art museum in town. I can spend hours in there. "You've lived here all your life?" he asks.

I nod. "For the most part. Did I hear correctly that your job is in Sweet Briar right now?"

"Yep. Have you heard about the new developments taking place there?"

"I have. It's going to be amazing. Sweet Briar's a cool, little town. I'd love to see it get more attention. Are you a part of it somehow?"

He winks. "I might be the one in charge of it."

Heart racing, I can feel the sweat running down my back. I didn't realize how important the man was. Not to mention, his job is to fix up my hometown. "That's amazing, Kai. Whatever you do, I hope it works."

"It will," he states in all seriousness. "I don't ever take on a project and fail. I'm working with a great team."

"Where did you move from?" I ask, turning the attention away from Sweet Briar.

"Malibu."

So that's why he has tanned skin. "Did you surf?"

He shows his white teeth again. "All the time. I got pretty good at it. What do you like to do for fun?"

"Well, I love to cook, obviously. And when I'm not doing that, I like to hike and be outdoors. That's what I was going to do today before you called."

His body turns to me. "You can still do that. I'll just go with you."

"You hike?" I ask, doubting it completely.

"I love it. Believe it or not, I was an eagle scout as a boy. My parents were poor so I grew up hiking and swimming in lakes for entertainment. I'll never forget the hiking trips I went on with my dad."

I can see the truth on his face. Maybe he's not the stuck up douche I thought he'd be. "Sounds like fun. If you don't mind, I'll take you to one of my favorite places."

He waves toward the road. "I'll go anywhere you take me. I don't have anything I have to do."

It feels crazy to take this man to my secret spot, but in a way, I'm excited to. I've never been able to take anyone there. "All right, but it's kind of a drive."

Sitting back in the seat, he almost looks like a normal guy. "I don't mind."

Our destination is a forty-minute drive outside of Portland, but it goes by quick. We talk about my job and what he has to do in Sweet Briar. The next thing I know we're in the trailhead parking lot to Looking Glass Falls.

Kai focuses on the sign, a smile lighting up his face. It's hard not to smile when he looks at me like that. "Hiking, huh? That's what you wanted to do on your afternoon off?"

I shrug. "I've had a lot on my mind. Being here helps me think."

We get out of my car and I tighten up my laces. He walks over to my side and I'm thankful he's in tennis shoes as well. "What's on your mind?"

I stand and we're so close I can feel the heat from his body. Tucking my hair behind my ear, I look up at him. "I don't want to bore you with my personal life. I'm sure there's other things more important to talk about."

His brows lift and I hurry past him to the trail. "Okay, I'll take the hint," he calls out behind me. It doesn't take him long to catch up to me. "Where does this trail lead to?"

I happy sigh escapes my lips. "To the most beautiful waterfall in the whole state. It's absolutely gorgeous."

"I miss seeing places like that," he confesses. "It's hard to when you work all the time."

"Is that why you're single?" I ask, sneaking a glance at him.

His smile slightly fades. "For the most part. I was seeing someone casually in Malibu, but when the Sweet Briar job came about, we decided to split ways."

"I can understand that."

"What about you?"

A laugh escapes my lips and I shake my head. "My life is complicated right now. I'm kind of involved with someone, only I'm not. I know it doesn't make any sense."

"Actually, it does," he cuts in.

"And then I ran into my ex at the store. He wants to go out some time."

"You're a very attractive woman, Dria. Any man would be happy to have you."

I playfully bump into his shoulder. The reaction comes out of nowhere, but Kai seems to find it amusing. "Thanks," I reply sweetly. The sound of the waterfall draws closer and I pick up my pace. "We're almost there."

Once we climb up the rock face and turn around the bend, the waterfall comes into view. It's twenty-five feet of pure bliss. The spray from the water coats my heated skin and it feels amazing. There's a large rock partway into the water so I take off my shoes to get there. Kai does the same and joins me. The rock is big enough for us both to spread out on.

Lying on my back, I lean up on my elbows and watch Kai skip rocks across the water. "How long will you stay in Portland?"

He reaches into the water for more rocks. "Until the job is done, probably a couple of years, depending on how it goes."

"What about settling down? Do you not want to stay in the same place and start a family? You have to be pushing thirty." It's a bold question, but I'm curious.

Chuckling, he skips another rock across the water and sits down. "And you're what, twenty-five?" I nod and he shrugs a shoulder. "One day I'll settle down ... when I meet the right woman."

"You will. I have faith."

His eyes lift straight to mine. "I have to say, you're different from any woman I've ever been with. It's so easy to talk to you, almost like I've always known you."

I wink. "I've been told that before. I tend to make friends easily."

"Hopefully, you'll consider me as one. I don't have any around here. Every time I move, I start all over."

I can't imagine that. "What about your family? Where do they live?"

With a heavy sigh, he throws the last of his rocks into the water. "Arizona. With my schedule, I see them maybe four times a year. It's hard. I miss them."

"At least, you get along with yours. My father and I don't exactly see eye to eye these days." I bite my tongue, hating that I even confided in him.

"Why not?"

"Doesn't matter," I answer with a shake of my head. "It's not something I want to talk about." Getting to my feet, I wade through the water back to my shoes. "We should probably get back. The sun will be going down soon."

By the expression on his face, he can tell he struck a nerve. The last thing I want to do is talk about my family drama with a man I barely know. When we get to the car, he rests his forearms on the roof and peers over at me. "I had a good time today. Do you think you'd like to grab dinner one night?" I open my mouth to say no, but he holds up his hands. "As friends. I can sense you're not ready for anything more than that. I'm not either if that makes you more comfortable."

Breathing a sigh of relief, I nod. "It does. Nothing against you, Kai, but I can't see anything happening between us. We're too different."

He shrugs. "I beg to differ." With one last grin, he gets in the car and shuts the door.

The butterflies I've been trying to deny come back with a vengeance. I can't let another man into my life.

SEVENTEEN

Kai

---

*Y*ou know when you first meet someone and there's something about the expression they hold in their eyes that keeps you intrigued? That's how I felt the other night when I met Dria. Her eyes alone held my attention. Then it was the way she'd smile when she was being spoken to, and then her spitfire attitude at the end of the night when I asked for her number.

But that wasn't the Dria I met the other day. No, the one who showed me around was different. She was stand-offish and cold. Almost as if something happened from when we met to when I showed up at her house. I don't know what happened to her in that small gap of time, but someone did a number of her.

She mentioned an ex, but she also mentioned that she was sort of seeing someone, but wasn't and it was complicated. That's how I liken my relationship to the woman at Society X. I mean, we're not technically seeing each other but we are engaging in sexual activity. And for fuck's sake, she gave me, a man she doesn't know, her virginity. That alone is enough to fuck both of us for a long time.

By all accounts I shouldn't text Dria. In fact, I should lose her number. She's probably wondering if I dropped off the face of the Earth. It's been a few days, and by a few I mean four to be exact. This is where that "do I text or call question" comes into play. I know she said she's not interested, which means back the fuck off, but I am and I can't shake the sense that I'm meant to know her, which makes me feel like a total ass for waiting this long.

I know there's a possibility that we'll run into each other at another one of Parker's gatherings, assuming he uses the same service, but I could ignore her. I could play it off as if we never met. Hell, I could even bring a date and show her what she's missing.

But I can't. There's something about her that I'm drawn to and I don't know what it is. I find myself thinking about her more than I should. We went on one date—which wasn't exactly a date—and she blew me off. That should be a sign to cut my losses and move on.

And yet, here I am looking at the text message box with my thumb poised and ready to send her a message. I have typed and retyped what I want to say to her so many times I've lost count. Never have I questioned myself so much about sending a simple text to a woman before. I don't want her to misconstrue my words or think I'm hounding her. For some odd reason, I genuinely like her and want to spend more time with her.

Maybe it's because she seems to know Sweet Briar and cared about the revitalization project. Or it's the fact that when I look at her, I feel like I've met her. I should've asked if she spent any time in California, maybe that is where we've crossed paths.

The message I have to her is generic, leaving plenty of room to open a conversation. That is what I want. I want to get her talking and see if she'll open up via text before I even tempt fate by asking her out again. Of course, with her ex in the picture and the sort of other man she's dating her social calendar is probably filling up fast. I erase the message I have and retype a new one:

Thank you for the hike. I'm sorry I haven't called or texted. Job is busy! I was wondering if you've ever been to California?

I quickly send the message and pocket my phone, turning my attention back to the job site. Everything is coming along smoothly. The concrete basement is in with the exterior walls going up. The construction crew that won the bid on the job has been working their tails off, in hopes of finishing early. If they do, they get a bonus—which is something Parker offered after he notified the company they won the bid. I should probably ask him if I get one, too. Not that I need one, but it's nice to be rewarded sometimes.

Every few minutes, I'm tempted to check my phone, but the ringer is on and I should hear if a message comes in. I haven't felt this anxious since Jenica started texting me about being in the club. I'm trying not to let it bother me that I haven't heard from her either. Stupidly, I checked my rating after the night in the dark room and it was good, so one would think my friend would set up another meeting ... but for what? Other than spanking, I can't think of a single thing we haven't done, so maybe there won't be another call. She got what she wanted or needed.

We both had needs that were fulfilled within those walls. Hers were a little more ... I don't even know. I still can't wrap my head around taking her virginity when I don't even know her name. In fact, it's weighing heavily on me. I need to know if she's okay and want to know if I hurt her in anyway. I fully went into the dark room expecting straight up sex, but wasn't prepared to hear those words.

It's hard for me to wrap my head around the fact that she had to use the club to what ... learn? Is that what she was doing? I try to think back to my blowjob. It was amazing. Definitely one of the best ones I have ever received. I would've never thought it was her first time. But when I went to return the favor, she was shy and timid, enough that I almost walked out of the room because nervousness was coming off of her in droves. I was nervous, too, though. I hated that I had regulated myself to seeking sexual companionship in a seedy club.

By the time lunch rolls around, my phone beeps. I can't even lie and say that I was completely casual about checking because I wasn't. I pulled my phone out of my pants so fast that it went flying across the floor. Pastor Larry was nice enough to pick it up and hand it back to me.

"Lady friend?" he asks, nodding toward the phone.

I glance quickly at the screen and see that it's from Dria. I can't keep the smile off my face even without knowing what her reply is. "A friend," I tell him. I hope I can call her that, if not more, if she allows us to hang out. The polite thing to do is to put my phone away, but I can't. I have to know.

Sorry, I had a catering job this morning You're welcome for the hike. Nope, never been to California. You'll have to tell me about it!

My internal fist is pumping while my brain is screaming

YES! She left it open for more conversation and a possible date. I know I can play it smooth and chat back but that's not me. I'm a go get 'em type, and when I see something or someone, as in this case, I go for it.

How about dinner, tonight? I'm almost done in Sweet Briar. I can pick you up at 7?

After I send her the text, I attach a few images of the job sites I've been at today so she can see the progress we're making. Putting my phone face down, I turn my attention to Pastor Larry and the women of the congregation.

"Tell us, Kai, are you fitting in?" one lady asks.

"Yes, I think so."

"Do you like Portland?" another inquires. "I find it too busy."

I take a quick drink of my water before answering. "I do like it, but I'm from the city. I do have to say though, I like Sweet Briar a lot and can see why Mr. Ward is so eager to help."

"We need more people like you and my daughter, putting down roots here. It's what's going to build this town back up," Pastor Larry adds.

"Oh yes, having Lexi here would be so pleasant. Have you met her yet, Kai?" another lady asks.

I shake my head. "No, sorry. I'm fairly busy."

"He has a lady friend, Martha," Pastor Larry says. I chuckle slightly at usage of "lady friend" and wonder what it's like to live with the old-fashioned rules. Hell, I don't know how men resisted women until marriage. By the time I was eighteen I was having sex with any willing woman and never even gave it a second thought when I was about

121

to lose my virginity at a party. It was more like a hurrah moment for me.

I'm well on my way home when Dria texts back, agreeing to dinner. Breaking the 'no texting and driving' law, I tell her that I'll pick her up and we'll go to a casual place. I don't want her stressing about what to wear.

As soon as I get home, I shower and make a reservation at a local restaurant that Parker suggested. I asked him for a place to take a casual date and he gave me a list. I don't know how long he and his wife have been married, but I do wonder if he was a player before he married Mia.

With the reservation made, I head over to Dria's. I'm a bit early so I circle the block a few times, checking out the houses in her neighborhood. Most of them are rundown, which for me makes a good investment. I have been thinking about getting into the flip market. It's profitable and I have the means and skills to get the job done. It also gives me something else to focus on while I'm in town.

Pulling up to Dria's with five minutes to spare, I rush to her door to get her. If anything, I'm a gentleman. I'll greet her at her door, open the car door, hold the door at the restaurant, and walk her to her door at night, even if this is our last date. I barely knock when she opens the door, standing there with a creamy yellow sundress on. In her hand she's holding a sweater, prepared for the cooler night ahead. But it's the way her hair is pulled up off her neck and her sun-kissed skin that has me at a loss for words. She's beautiful and I know that without a doubt I will pursue her if she allows me to.

I clear my throat. "Sorry, tongue tied. You look lovely," I tell her as I offer her my arm. She steps out of her house and makes sure her door is locked before placing her arm in mine.

"Thank you, you dress up nicely," she replies with a smile.

"I can put the top up," I offer as I help her into the car.

"No, I think I'd like to feel the wind in my hair."

I'd like to feel my fingers in your hair, but I don't say that to her. Instead, I rush around to the other side and get in. I take the back roads to head toward downtown so I can avoid the freeway. I'd rather sit in stop and go traffic with Dria as long as possible.

At the restaurant, talk is limited. This isn't exactly the intimate place I was hoping for. There's a band and it's rather loud. We eat mostly in silence because neither of us is fond of yelling at each other to have a conversation. I'll be sure to point this out to Parker when I see him next.

After dinner, I take her hand and walk her toward the waterfront. I'm not ready for the date to end. Surprisingly she doesn't let go, but I'm not willing to read anything into it. Dria points out different sites and talks about how in early June the Navy ships will come in and dock for Fleet Week, and how there will be numerous celebrations throughout the downtown area. She tells me about the Saturday market and how it's the best place to get fresh vegetables and homemade goods.

"We should go tomorrow," I suggest. Anything I can do to spend more time with her.

"I can pick you up," she tells me to which I nod eagerly. "It's only from ten to five, so we should probably go early."

When I drop her off, I kiss her cheek. My lips linger there for a moment, mostly because she feels so damn familiar. Everything about her seems memorable and I can't put my finger on it. She's definitely one of a kind and must have a doppelganger out in the world that I have come across before.

"I'll see you around ten," she says. "That way we can spend the day there."

I quickly text my address and kiss her again because I simply can't get enough of her. Maybe tonight was a starting point for us. She didn't seem agitated or stressed out. Dria wasn't the same as she was when we went hiking last week, and for that I'm thankful. She didn't fill my night by telling me she wasn't interested in anything. In fact, she sort of led me to believe something could happen.

All I know is that tomorrow, I plan to be the same Kai that I am right now. I won't push her, but you can bet your ass I'm going to flirt like there's no tomorrow. Before I pull away from her curb, I text Jenica and ask her to set something up with the woman I've been with. Deep down, I'm hoping Jenica comes back and says she's not interested, this way I can move on without this quasi-romance looming over my head.

EIGHTEEN

Alexandria

I'm starting to think I needed the break. It's been days since my night in the dark room and as the time passes, so does my heartbreak. Don't get me wrong, not hearing from the club made me a little upset, but it's probably for the best. I no longer wear my Society X necklace. It's hidden in my underwear drawer at home.

I backed off from Kai because I thought there might've been something between me and my mystery man. It's probably a good thing there's not. Losing my virginity to someone I don't know isn't something to be proud of, but I wouldn't trade the experience for anything else.

Taking Kai to the Saturday market is going to be fun. I haven't been to it in a long time. The GPS leads me to an expensive apartment complex in the city. I drive around until I find his unit. It's definitely bigger than my entire house.

I check my makeup and run a hand through my hair before getting out of the car. Kai opens the door before I even knock. His smile sends butterflies through my stomach. With his hair underneath a baseball cap and dressed in a pair of jeans and a T-shirt, I can't help but think he looks like a normal guy. Not one who makes a gazillion dollars a year.

He stands in the doorway smiling. "Did you want to come in or should we go?"

I nod toward my car. "We should probably go. It gets really crowded later."

"All right," he says, locking the door. "Let's go." We get in my car and head toward the market. "Thanks for seeing me again. I honestly didn't think you'd want to."

I shrug. "I've had a few days to think. I never should've said we were too different to work. There's nothing wrong with being friends."

"Exactly," he agrees, giving me that seductive grin of his. "We can always figure out everything else as it comes."

I smile back. "I'm good with that." There are cars everywhere, but I'm lucky enough to find a spot that won't make us walk a mile. My arm brushes against Kai's as we walk and shivers run down my skin. The next thing I know, he has my hand in his as we cross the street. It feels so good.

"This is awesome," he says, glancing at all the different vendor booths.

"Wait until you try the cinnamon and sugar roasted almonds. They're over in that area." I point at the far side of the market.

My stomach growls just thinking about them and Kai laughs. "Sounds good to me." His fingers tighten around mine and I smile. We slowly meander through the first row of vendors and I'm glad we're taking our time. I don't want the day to end. "Why did you agree to come out with me today?" he asks.

I try to ignore the pang in my chest. "Remember when I told you I had a complicated relationship?" He nods, his brows furrowed with concern. "I think it's over. I felt guilty for dating you while I was kind of seeing someone else."

His eyes widen. "So that's over now?"

I shrug. "I think so. But aren't you kind of seeing someone, too?"

"Not anymore." We walk over to the river and lean against the rails. The wind whips by us, blowing a strand of hair into my face. Kai gently brushes it away, and I lean into his touch. It feels so familiar. "Now that we're not being held back anymore, what do you say about maybe taking this a step further?"

As he pulls me closer, I bite my lip. "What do you have in mind?"

His head dips lower, his mouth so close to mine. I close my eyes and hold my breath as he kisses me. Only when he pulls back do I breathe. "I enjoyed that," I whisper.

Cupping my cheeks, he murmurs against my lips. "Just one more."

Before he can kiss me, someone calls my name. "Alexandria!"

Kai steps back and my head jerks to the side. My high school sweetheart, Matt, waves and heads our way, his arm around a pretty brunette. I was going to tell Kai my full name, but it looks like I don't have to now.

"Matt," I call out and wave back.

Letting his date go, he hugs me and puts his arm back around her. With his other hand, he holds it out to Kai. "Hi, I'm Matt, one of Alex's friends. We grew up together."

Kai shakes his hand. "Kai."

Matt nods. "I know. I recognize your face. You're working on the Sweet Briar project, right? My father told me all about it."

Kai puts his arm around my waist and it's the first time

I realize the kind of man I'm with. He's easily recognizable and definitely high profile. A part of me is exhilarated about being with him, but the other part is terrified. Dating a man in the public eye will put my life in the public as well.

"That's me," Kai says happily. "Sweet Briar is a special place."

Matt squeezes the woman's shoulders. "Yes, it is. It's where I met Sarah." Clearing his throat, he looks at her and then at me. "Sarah, this is Alexandria."

I shake her hand and she smiles. "It's nice to meet you," I tell her.

"Likewise. I like meeting Matt's friends."

Kai holds me tighter and I don't even attempt to look up at his face. "How did you two meet?" I ask.

They both laugh and I can't help but join in. I'm relieved to know Matt is with someone else. He was the other obstacle standing in the way of Kai and me. Sarah proceeds to tell me about how she was stranded on the side of the road in a pile of mud. Matt rescued her, but not before they both ended up covered in it, trying to push her car out.

"Sounds hilarious," I say, meeting Matt's gaze. "I'm glad you're happy."

His eyes flick over to Kai's and then back to me. "You too. Maybe we'll see you both around Sweet Briar sometime." Hand in hand, they stroll back up to the market.

"Alexandria, huh?" Kai teases, turning me to face him. "Now I know your real name."

I throw my arms around his neck. "I was going to tell you."

"Sure about that?"

I roll my eyes. "Yes. Everyone calls me Alex or Alexandria. Dria was something I came up with at the last minute. I didn't think anything would happen between us."

"What else are you keeping from me?" he asks.

"Nothing. I promise I was going to tell you. From now on, I won't keep anything from you."

He holds me close. "Good. I think we have something here."

"Me too ... but I think we're missing something."

His brows lift. "What?"

"Almonds."

We walk back up to the market toward the food vendors. "With you being a master chef, wouldn't you be able to make them yourself?"

"Oh no," I laugh. "It's much better to get them here." The line is always long for those amazing almonds, but when we finally purchase our bag, the lady hands it to Kai. I try to reach for some, but he hurries away, holding the bag in the air. "So help me God," I shout, "you better give those to me now." The people around us are snickering and watching us.

Kai taps his lips. "Kiss me and I'll give you a bite."

I kiss him quickly. "All right, I did it."

"Open your mouth." He places an almond on my tongue and I chew it quickly. It tastes so good. I reach for the bag, but he still keeps it away from me.

"You're playing on dangerous ground, Kai," I warn teasingly.

He nods toward a bench and we sit down. "Answer my questions and I'll give you an almond each time."

Crossing my arms over my chest, I purse my lips, but in truth, I'm amused. He's not at all like I thought he'd be. "If I answer your questions, you have to answer mine," I counter.

"Deal. What's your favorite color?" he asks first.

"Green. Yours?"

"Blue" He winks and holds out the almond bag. Grabbing a couple, I toss them in my mouth. "What are you most afraid of?"

I shiver. "Spiders. My neighbor used to throw them on me when we were kids. You?"

"Clowns. I blame it on *It*, the movie."

We both burst out laughing. That movie scared the shit out of me as well. He hands me the bag of almonds and we both stuff a handful into our mouths. "I never thought a man like you could be humorous," I admit.

"Most people think I'm a douche, and most women think I'm all about the sex."

"And you're not?" I ask.

He turns his serious gaze to mine. "No. Don't get me wrong, sex is nice, but it's not all I want. Most of the time, it's all the women want from me. Well, that and my money."

"That's the last thing I want."

He laughs. "Which one? My money or sex?"

I smack his arm. "Money."

"Oh, so there's still a possibility of the sex?"

I can feel the blood rush to my cheeks. "We'll see," I say, tossing an almond into my mouth. "I'm not making any promises." Although, I'd really love to have sex again. It'd be nice to actually see the person I'm making love to. I can just imagine how amazing it would be to see Kai above me, his hips rocking against mine.

"How about we cook dinner together tonight? We can talk and do whatever else you want to do. Hell, we can play board games if it makes you happy. I'm not ready to end the day."

Excitement bubbles in my veins and I'm just about to say yes when my phone vibrates in my pocket. It's done that a few times during the day, but I ignored it. "Hold on. Let me see who this is," I say quickly. There's a missed call from my mother, but then there's a text from someone I wasn't expecting... Jared.

Good afternoon, Alexandria. You've been invited back to the dark room by your partner. Would you like to accept?

I can hear my heart pounding in my ears. Kai rubs a hand over my leg, grabbing my attention. Guilt overwhelms me when I look in his eyes. I want to spend time with him, but I thought my time at the club was over.

"What do you say?" Kai murmurs. "Dinner tonight?"

I squeeze my phone, hoping like hell I'm not making a wrong decision. "Can I have a raincheck? Something just came up."

With a heavy sigh, he nods. "Sure. We'll figure out another time."

Stomach in knots, we walk to my car and get in. I feel horrible for choosing the club over Kai, but I have to figure out what to do.

NINETEEN

Kai

---

*T*he car ride back to my place is done in silence. The idea that I'd invite her in and give Dria a tour of my place has long since passed. Every time I look at her, her eyes are focused on the road ahead and her lower lip is pulled between her teeth. Whatever came up has completely ruined the mood for the day.

I thought I was making progress. We were flirting back and forth, and while I may have initiated the contact by reaching for her hand, she didn't let go or squirm away. In fact, she stepped closer to me, leaning into me to point out certain vendors. When the opportunity to kiss her came up, I didn't hesitate. Hell, I couldn't. I would've been an idiot for not taking the chance.

And now I'm standing in the parking lot of my building, watching the red tail light of her Camry disappear. Part of me wants to believe that it's a family emergency, but deep down I know it's the mystery guy. Wherever he was, he's back and taking my Dria with him. *Fucking bastard.*

As soon as I open the door to my apartment, the instant smell of flowers hits my senses. I bought them to decorate, to show Dria that I'm not living in a bachelor pad, that I actually have some taste. The bottle of wine I started to chill is sitting in the ice bucket, mocking me.

"So much for trying," I say to the bottle. I leave it there and opt for a beer instead. No man should drink wine when they're alone. It doesn't seem right.

Sitting down on my couch, I prop my feet up on my coffee table, have my cold beer in one hand and the remote in the other. I surf between the sports channels, hoping to find a game that interests me. When my phone chimes, I think it's Dria, only to find a text from Jenica.

Your partner agreed. Play room. She would like to try a fetish – spanking. Can you be here in 30?

My heart sinks at the word spanking. I am not keen on hitting a woman, and while I know it's not the same, spanking doesn't appeal to me, not even during sex. I'm tempted to tell Jenica no, but I asked for this to be setup and knowing that my lady friend was a virgin until last week, I don't want to disappoint her. She needed something and I was the one who ended up giving it to her. I don't want to let her down.

I dump my beer in the sink and rush off to the club after texting Jenica back. Usually I would like more time so I can shower and feel clean, but thirty minutes doesn't give me enough time.

When I pull in my anxiety level is at an all-time high. What if I hit her too hard or not hard enough? Do I use my hand or a paddle? The one time I spanked a woman was during sex. She liked it rough, but her definition of rough and mine were vastly different. She wanted welts on her ass and handprints left around her neck. I finished my deed and got my ass out of her apartment. That freaky shit isn't for me.

Jenica is there to meet me at the door. I half smile when I see her, but she's full on happy. "Let me take you to the room."

Oh joy, can you please? I follow her down the hall, tempted to ask her what's going on in the viewing room. My membership fee allows me to go in there, but I haven't been tempted until now. Maybe I need some live action porn to get me over this funk or whatever it is that I'm feeling toward this woman. Unfortunately for me, I'm out of time because the play room door is staring me straight in the face.

"There's an assortment of toys that you can use on your partner. She won't be able to see you and she indicated that she'd like sex with anal penetration."

Jenica smiles and disappears down the hall before the words register in my mind. Anal penetration. Is that supposed to be a toy I stick up her ass or my finger? Fuck, why isn't there a rulebook with this place?

The door opens and I step in and slip off my shoes without looking at my partner. When I finally do, my heart sinks a little, but my cock starts dancing around as if he's won the lottery.

Her ass is straight up in the air and her ankles are tied the posts on the table. I can't believe I'm about to do this, and while I know it's to please her, you can bet I won't be asking for this in return.

Next to her is an assortment of toys that I can use. Different size paddles, whips, floggers, and something that is shaped like a heart. *That's cute.* I can leave heart welts all over her backside. And there are the butt plugs. So at least I know she wants something shoved up her ass. *Perfect. Just great*.

She clears her throat, getting my attention. Her ass shimmies in the air, causing me to step back. Tilting my head, I look at her backside and her legs. Something seems off. When she grunts, I know this isn't my partner. The woman I have been with is shy and reserved. She would never shake her ass or grunt to get my attention, and I can't imagine she would bend over a table like this, bare-assed so I can spank her.

Stepping away from the table, I slip my shoes back on and press the button to leave the room. By the time the door opens, Jenica is there and she doesn't seem pleased. "What's wrong?" she asks.

"That," I say, pointing toward the room, "isn't the woman I have been with."

"How could you possibly know, Kai? You're not allowed to speak to the clientele. It's in the contract you signed."

"We aren't speaking, but I can tell. A man knows things and that woman isn't the same one."

Jenica pulls out her phone and presses some buttons. "I'm afraid it is. You need to go back in there."

I shake my head. "The woman I've been with is inexperienced. The one in the room, her demeanor says otherwise."

"I'm sorry you feel that way, but we don't make mistakes here."

I glance back at the door and know that I'm right. "I'm sorry, I can't."

"But Kai—"

"No, listen. When I filled out that application, I did it so you'd leave me alone. My friend brought me here for lunch that day. I had no idea what this place was. I put things down on that form that I would never do to a woman, and spanking is one of them. That's not who I am and that certainly isn't the woman I requested. I'm sorry, but I can't give that woman what she wants right now."

With that I leave the club with Jenica calling after me. I don't care if they revoke my membership and ban me for life at this point. I trust my instincts and those are telling me to run.

By the time I get home, I'm depressed. I was looking forward to seeing the woman tonight, and hopefully learning something new about her, but as my luck would have it, I'm going to drown my sorrow in a case of local brew and figure out how to cancel my membership.

I hate the thought of canceling and never seeing my lady friend again, but I can't stomach going back there. That voodoo shit messed with my head one too many times, and I'm better off focusing on Sweet Briar, and maybe Dria if her mystery asshole will ever leave her alone.

Speaking of Dria, I pull out my phone and call her. It's been hours since she dropped me off, and while I know I shouldn't call her, I can't help myself.

The phone rings four times and I'm about to hang up when I hear her come on. "Hello," she croaks out. I sit up quickly, jostling my beer and spilling some on my shirt.

"Dria?"

"Hey, Kai."

The sound of my name coming from her lips is such a turn on. I want to ask her to say it over and over again, but I refrain.

"Are you crying?"

She sniffles and tells me no. I think about calling her out on her little white lie, but I don't want her to hang up.

"Want me to come over?" I ask.

She laughs. "No, I'm fine."

"Yeah that's probably best. I've had a little too much to drink anyway."

"Are you drunk?"

I hold my bottle out as if she can see, and eye the other five or six sitting on my coffee table. "Maybe," I say. "I don't know because I haven't moved in a while."

"Perhaps I should join you."

"Yes! Yes, you should. The beautiful Alexandria should come over so I can take care of her." She laughs again and it's music to my ear. "Tell me why you're crying," I plead.

"It's a long story, Kai, and not one that I'm proud of."

"Does it have to do with that text you received? It was from him, right?"

Dria sighs. "It was, sort of. I don't know how to explain things between us. I thought ... well, I don't know what I thought, but after tonight it's definitely over."

"He didn't like your almonds, huh?"

"No, I guess he didn't."

"I like your almonds," I tell her, while trying not to laugh. Who knew that the nut could become a sexual innu-endo? "I had fun earlier, Dria. A lot of fun. I'd like to see you again. Preferably on the other side of my door in about thirty minutes?"

"Oh, Kai. I can't even believe you're on the phone with me right now after the way I treated you. I should've never looked at my phone. I'm sorry I did, and I'm sorry I ruined our day. It was very selfish of me."

"And you're on your way over?" I hedge.

Dria laughs. "And what would we do while I was there?"

"I can think of a hundred things we could do. Most of them revolve around kissing because let's face it, I didn't get enough of your lips today. Or we could watch a movie, snuggle on my couch, finish off my case of beer or play Twister."

"Do you actually have Twister?"

"Uh ... not the board game version."

"Oh," she says, suddenly quiet.

"Seriously, though. I want to see you again."

"Okay," she replies, causing me to sit up even more.

"Yeah? Good. I know this is going to sound stupid, but I'd like to make you dinner."

"That's not stupid at all," she says.

"But it is. You're a chef. I'm sure you can cook circles around me."

"No one besides my mom has ever cooked for me, Kai. So I would really like that."

Dria and I stay on the phone for an hour while I sober up. I ask her again if she wants to talk about her night, but she changes the subject quickly. Whatever happened this evening has really put her in a funk, but I'm determined to help her get over him. One home-cooked meal at a time.

TWENTY

Alexandria

---

*I*f there was ever a clusterfuck of a night it was tonight. I dump Kai for my mystery guy, only to get my heart broken. I thought about calling Dani to tell her what happened, but I couldn't even stomach the embarrassment. I'm done with Society X. There's no way I can ever show my face there again. My heart was crushed, but maybe it's for the best. Unfortunately, all I can think about as I drive to Kai's is how my night in the dark room ended.

I show up at the club and Jared takes me to the dark room. I'm nervous to be in there, but I take off my clothes and lie on the bed. A part of me is torn because I have feelings for Kai, and yet, I'm there about to be with another man. The more time that ticks by, I question why I'm there. When the door opens, I'm shocked to see a shine of light as well. I look up, thinking I'll see my mystery man, but instead, it's Jared. Clearing his throat, he directs his gaze at the floor.

"I'm sorry, Alexandria. Your partner never showed up."

The world crashes all around me and I jump out of bed, rushing past him into the dressing room. I throw on my clothes and leave, never once looking back.

Tears stream down my cheeks and I angrily wipe them away. How dare he ask me to the dark room and not show? My mind is set. I never want to be with him again. When I get to Kai's apartment, I can smell the scent of garlic and oregano outside the door. My stomach growls. Maybe I can eat my way out of a broken heart. Before I can knock, the door opens. Kai gets one look at my face and his smile fades. He pulls me into his arms.

"He's not worth it, Dria."

Burying my head in his chest, I breathe him in. "Call me Alex," I whisper.

He rubs my back. "Alex it is then."

"I'm so very sorry. Please forgive me for today."

Clutching my arms, he pulls me away, his expression serious. "There's nothing to apologize for. We both made mistakes today."

My brows furrow. "What have you done?"

"Nothing worth talking about," he replies with a shake of his head. "All that matters is that it's over and we're here now."

I nod, even though my heart still hurts. "The food smells delicious. I'm sensing Italian."

He grins. "Chicken Parmesan. Then for dessert, I have a shit ton of chocolate ice cream. Or if you prefer chocolate frosting we can run down to the store."

"The ice cream's fine," I giggle.

Taking my hand, Kai leads me into his apartment. His brown leather couch and chair probably cost more than all the furniture in my house. When I sit down on the couch, he pours us both a glass of white wine.

"I think we both could use it."

I scoff. "That's an understatement."

The wine goes down like water and I can already feel it

coursing through my veins. Kai sits down beside me, but he keeps a little space between us. "Care to talk about it?"

Grabbing the bottle of wine, I fill my glass to the rim. "There's really nothing to say. He wants to meet me and then he doesn't show up." I gulp down more of the wine. "Doesn't matter anyway. It was stupid to even consider it. What we had wasn't real." Taking a deep breath, I gaze into his eyes. "Not like what we have between us. Spending time with you today felt amazing."

He reaches over and tucks a strand of hair behind my ear. "I agree. I'm just hoping you'll drop those walls of yours and let me in. I don't like sharing those I care about with other men."

Hearing those words sends a flood of warmth through my body. I've never had a man want me all to himself. Then again, I've never had anything serious before. "What about you?" I counter. "If you don't want to share me, does that go for you as well?"

"Is that what you want?"

For a second, I contemplate it all. Am I really ready for a commitment after I just lost my virginity to another man? "I'll let you know," I say sweetly. "I think I just need a little more time."

His lips pull back in a sly grin. "Okay, I get it. It's probably for the best. There's no need to rush." A part of me wants to give in, but my heart's not ready for it. He pats my leg and stands. "Let's eat. I'm starving." He takes my hand and I follow him into the kitchen. Everything smells so amazingly good. "Have a seat," he says, pulling out a chair. After fixing my plate, he sets it down in front of me. When he sits down, I can't help but stare at him in awe. His brows lift. "Everything okay?"

I glance down at my food and it looks delicious. "It's more than okay. I'm just shocked is all."

"Of what?"

"You," I reply. "I'm not used to a man serving me. I grew up with my mother doing everything for my father. The man doesn't even make his own dinner plate." I stuff a bite of chicken in my mouth and it practically melts it's so good.

Kai shook his head. "That's kind of fucked up. My father never expected my mother to take care of him."

I shrug. "My mother doesn't mind doing the things she does, but I knew long ago I didn't want to be like that. It's one of the reasons I left. If my parents had their way, I'd be married with ten kids."

Kai bursts out laughing. "Sounds like my mother. She's dying to have grandkids."

"Is she the one who taught you how to cook?" I ask, finishing the rest of my food.

He nods. "My father used to travel a lot with work. We lived not far from the schools, and I'd walk home every day. When my mother got home, she was always tired, so I'd help her fix dinner." He smiles down at my plate. "Obviously, I did something right. Maybe I could come to work for you when you start your own business."

I snort. "I wish. I refuse to even try to get a business loan until Sandy retires."

"I understand. You value your relationship with her. That's rare in the world today. The people I work with would turn on me in a heartbeat if given the opportunity."

"I'm sorry to hear that. I'm hoping Dani and Adrienne will come work for me when I do get my own business. They're like family."

Getting up, Kai takes our plates to the sink. "I'm glad

you have friends like that. Most of mine have gone different ways over the years."

"You have me now."

He smiles. "That's all I need." He stares down at me, and then nods toward the living room. "Why don't we relax for a while and maybe watch a movie?"

"As long as it's a comedy. I don't want to cry anymore."

Putting his arm around me, he leads me to the couch. "Trust me, there'll be no more crying tonight." We sit down and I take off my shoes so I can face him. He does the same, and our knees slightly touch as we look at each other. His eyes darken and it's almost like I can sense his need for me. My own desire feels like it's going to explode right out of me.

"Want to know what I like most about you?" he asks, sliding his hands into my lap.

I peer down at our entwined fingers. "What?"

"Look at me," he whispers. I do as he says and he moves closer, his lips incredibly close to mine. It's the first time I've gotten a good look at all the different colors in his eyes. They're mesmerizing. "I like how I feel when I'm around you. I can't explain it." Closing the distance, he kisses me gently. "Even when I kiss you, it just feels right."

It makes no sense, but I feel the same way. "I know what you mean."

He kisses me again, and this time, it's deeper, harder. His hands slide up my body to my face, and the next thing I know, I'm lying on my back with him above me. Looking up at his face, I can just imagine doing the same thing while he makes love to me. My whole body tightens just thinking about it ... but I'm not ready. Placing his forehead to mine, Kai kisses me one last time.

"Sorry," he murmurs. "I got carried away. I know you want to take things slow."

I palm his cheek. "I do, but I thoroughly enjoyed that."

His arousal presses into my thigh. "Me too. What do you say we watch a movie and just lay here together all night?"

"All night? Think you can keep your hands to yourself for that long?"

He kisses me again and winks. "I promise not to touch you ... much."

TWENTY-ONE

Kai

————

$\mathcal{M}$y promise to not touch Alex (much) has been the worst mistake of my life. It's been about two weeks since I made her dinner after what started off as an amazing day that quickly turned to shit, only to redeem itself by the night's end. I think I have lost count of how many hand jobs I've given myself either after she's left my place or I've left hers. Believe me, the drive back from her house to my apartment isn't enough to curb the ache I feel for her.

I'm trying to be good and respect her wishes, but damn it's hard. Our flirt game is strong and Alex is sexy without being sexy. It's little things like when she comes over after work and her hair is down, it'll cover her face after I've given her a compliment, which then gives me the best excuse to touch her, to move her hair behind her ear.

Or the time when I went to her place for dinner and walked in on her wearing these ridiculously short shorts and dancing in the kitchen. I stood there and watched her hips move to the music, imagining what it's going to be like when we're finally intimate.

And that is what I'm hoping for, the intimacy. This woman drives me insane with her pouty lips, rosy pink cheeks, and long eyelashes that hide the prettiest green eyes I have ever seen. Alex has everything going for her in the looks department, but that bastard mystery man she was seeing really fucked up her head and heart.

Every day I chip away at that wall she's put up, determined to show her that I'm a man worth the risk. I can easily see myself falling in love with her. Hell, I might already be there, but I'm definitely holding back and protecting my heart. There's a nagging voice in the back of my head that is warning me, preparing me for when this mystery man shows back up and rocks the foundation Alex and I are building.

Since my fateful night in at Society X, I have been devoting my free time, and a bit of work time, to Alex. I've deleted Jenica's number and refuse to go to lunch with Bryant unless I'm the one picking the restaurant. If I never see or hear of that place, it'll be too soon.

Even thinking about it now makes me shudder. I can't believe I even entertained the idea in the first place, especially now that I've met Alex. That's all I needed was to get out of my apartment and be social. Resorting to paid sexual action has never been my thing, and I can guarantee it'll never happen again.

I shut my laptop, packing it away before heading out onto the job site. The apartment complex is coming along swimmingly, and much faster than I had anticipated. Usually we're looking at a year or longer when we build something like this, but this crew is working sun up to sun down to get this done. It'll still be nine months or so, but I couldn't be happier with the progress.

Down the way, the shopping plaza renovation is almost complete. Bryant is a marketing genius and got us in touch with one of the hottest commercial real estate agents in the state. Susan Mason has been a shark when it comes to finding the right clientele, and has been able to secure multiple contracts, with two moving in starting next week.

It's taken me a bit to accept that the job with Ward Enterprises was for the best, but now that I see everything coming to fruition, I'm glad I did. Of course, dating or what-ever I'm doing with Alex doesn't hurt either. Honestly, meeting her has changed my outlook on Portland a little bit. It doesn't seem so drab and overpopulated.

As soon as I arrive back at the office, Parker knocks on my door. "Got a minute?"

"Yeah, of course," I say as I set my stuff down. If it were anyone else, I'd go behind my desk and sit, but not with Parker. He's a big guy and the boss, which equals him scaring the shit out of me. And because of this, I sit on the edge of my desk, which is really the corner and I'm jabbing myself in the ass.

"Mia and I went out to Sweet Briar last night to see how things were going. I have to say, Kai, I'm impressed."

"Thank you."

Parker shakes his head and instantly my heart jumps into my throat. Isn't being impressed a compliment? "I knew you could do it, but you're exceeding my expectations. With that said, word will spread fast about your ability and I'm afraid to lose you. I have other projects in the pipeline that I'd love to discuss with you when you're ready."

"That'd be great," I tell him even though mentally I haven't committed myself to Portland past the two-year mark.

"I have one request though," he says. I nod for him to continue. "When the job offers start rolling in, give me a chance to match them. You're an asset to Ward Enterprises, and as far as I'm concerned, irreplaceable."

My mouth drops open and closes quickly as I try to find the words to tell him how grateful I am. I think my lack of speech is the perfect indication for him because he smiles, then leaves my office. Even as I watch him retreat, I still can't make my brain work. I'm in complete shock that I have made that good of impression on Parker. Maybe Portland is where I need to stay.

My phone dings, finally spurring my now achy legs to move. I rifle though my bag, only to realize it's in my pocket.

"Hello?" I don't bother looking to see who it is.

"Hey, so I was wondering if you'd like to come over for dinner?" Alex asks.

The answer is yes. It'll always be yes, but that's all we do, and while I love spending time with her inside our walls, I want to take her on a date.

"You know I do, but I was thinking we could take a picnic down to the waterfront and watch the fireworks tonight?"

"Oh, that sounds lovely, Kai. I'll bring everything."

"I'll grab the wine. Meet at my place at six?"

"I'll be there." She hangs up without a good-bye, which this day and age seems to be a lost art. Even my mother will randomly hang up. She tells me it's because she doesn't like saying "good-bye" because it feels final. I get it. I know she misses me, and I'm due for a visit. With the Sweet Briar project just starting though, I don't know if I'll be able to make it happen.

I decide to stay in the office and finish up a few

contracts. Usually once a project starts, paperwork gets pushed off to the side and I find myself scrabbling to get contractors paid or contracts signed. I don't want anything to slip through the cracks on this one.

By chance I look up at the clock and realize I only have five minutes to get home. There is no way I'm going to make it. I rush out of the office with my phone attached to my ear, praying Alex is running late. My call goes to voicemail. I call again and again, with the result being the same each time.

"Fuck," I yell as I reach my car. I drive out of the garage as fast as I can, which isn't easy with the turns, but I do my best. Of course, traffic would be backed up because why would the universe throw me a fucking bone? She's already fragile from that other guy and here I am, beyond late for our date.

By the time I pull into my complex, I'm an hour late. Thankfully though, her car is there, except she's not it, which means she's likely sitting on my steps. I rush toward my place, taking the steps two at a time, coming to a halt when I turn the corner and find her sitting there.

Alex looks at me, with tears in her eyes, breaking my heart. "Babe," I say, giving her a pet name without even thinking about what I'm doing. "I'm so sorry. I lost track of time."

She nods, but her eyes don't meet mine. I climb the steps slowly, unsure how to proceed. My ex knew that I kept late hours and would often call and remind me of our plans. I shouldn't have expected Alex to do that. I should've set a reminder on my phone, but I didn't and it looks like I've fucked up.

I approach her slowly, waiting to see what she's going to

do. Reaching out, I touch her hand, thankful that she doesn't pull away. "You said you were seeing someone when we first started hanging out."

"Yes, but it was ... I don't know what it was, Alex—"

"Is she why you're late?" she asks, looking at me with tears running down her face.

"God no," I say, cupping her cheeks. "I haven't seen her since the night I met you at the Ward party. Believe me, I was working and I lost track of time. I'll happily take you back to my office and ask security if you want. I will never lie to you, Alex."

Her hands grip my wrist and her eyes turn expectant. I lean forward and kiss her, brushing my lips across her slowly until she responds by opening her mouth and welcoming me in. Standing, she presses her body to mine, and we try to maneuver the rest of the way into my apartment.

"Your stuff," she says, breaking the kiss. As much as I would love to say fuck it, I can't. All my work is in there, and losing it is not an option. I quickly grab my bag and her picnic basket and bring them inside, tossing them down and kicking the door shut. She's my priority right now and I hate the fact that I had to stop kissing her.

Alex is where I left her, but still looking unbelievably sad. I don't know how to fix this or her for that matter, but I'm willing to try. Pushing her hair behind over her shoulder, I place a kiss just below her ear. The small intake of breath isn't lost on me in the least as I continue down her neck, pushing her shirt out of the way so I can kiss the tender flesh of her collarbone.

Her fingers dive into my hair as she tilts her neck to give me full access to her creamy skin. The shirt she is wearing is a V-neck, giving me the perfect path to follow. I know I'm tempting fate, but I don't care right now. With my arm around her waist, I lead toward my bedroom, anxious to have her laid out on my bed. I've only been dreaming about her for weeks, and maybe just maybe she'll let me touch her.

My lips reclaim hers. Tongues dance together. And I'm undoing my button down, hoping that she'll put her gentle fingers on my skin. Usually during our make-out sessions she'll slide her hand under my shirt, but keeps them firmly on my back. I want to feel her touch me, explore me, and have her make me hers.

We reach my bed, and she sits once the back of her knees touch. I don't even hesitate as I lift her shirt over her head. Fuck, the sight of her of in her navy blue bra turns me on. I want to reach for the clasp and undo her bra, but I don't know if she's ready.

Alex looks up at me and I nod toward my pillows. She moves back without even looking, making way for me to crawl toward her. I center myself over her, letting her feel what she does to me. Her eyes close as her fingers dig into my back. If this is a sign to come, she's going to be fucking amazing in bed.

Fuck, I want to be inside of her, to feel her body wrapped around mine. I recapture her lips, kissing her deeply and start dry humping her. She moans, and widens her legs so I can fit better. My bare skin rests against hers, the lace of her bra scratching me. Pulling back, I look at her swollen lips and smile before sliding down her body until I'm eye level with her breasts.

My finger traces along the pattern, watching as her skin pebbles in anticipation. I pull the cup aside, ready to take her in my mouth, but her hand stops me.

I look up and meet her gaze. "Not ready?" I ask.

She shakes her head. I respect her wishes and move back up to her body and resume kissing her, pretending that everything is okay. Unfortunately, it'll be another hand job for me tonight.

TWENTY-TWO

Alexandria

"*G*irl, you need to give me some updates." Dani nudges me in the side. There's flour on her cheeks and it makes me laugh.

"Updates about what?" I ask, knowing very well she's curious about Kai.

She rolls her eyes. "Have you told Kai about you losing your virginity in the club?"

Slapping a hand to her mouth, I glance around the room. Luckily, Sandy didn't hear her. "No," I grumble, whispering the words. "I don't plan on it either."

Adrienne walks by, carrying two apple pies, and sets them on the counter. "I don't blame you. He doesn't need to know everything."

"Exactly," I agree. "He's not the kind of guy to do what I did. After being dumped in the dark room by myself, it makes me regret ever going in the first place."

Smile fading, Dani runs a hand soothingly down my arm. "I can't imagine how you felt after that. It's a good thing you're done with that place. Now you have an amazing boyfriend with lots of money."

"That's not all it's about," Adrienne chides. "My husband doesn't make a lot money, but I love him all the same."

I was never one to care about material things. Maybe it's because my family didn't shower me with gifts. I grew up with the bare minimum. Granted, I'm glad I was brought up in a humble household. It makes me appreciate the good things I have now.

Sandy walks over and pats Dani and I on the back. "Figured I'd remind you girls in case you forgot."

"About what?" I ask, glancing at her over my shoulder.

Her lips purse. "My niece's wedding. Surely, you remembered you all have the day off."

Sheepishly, Dani smiles and nods her head. "Of course, we didn't forget. However, I'm still shocked *we're* not catering it. Does she not like our food?"

Laughing, Sandy waves her off. "Rayna loves our food. She thought it was best to hire another company so that I didn't have to work at hers. That way I can enjoy the wedding. Plus, we have family coming in from out of town. It'd be good to catch up with them."

"I bet she's excited," I reply.

Sandy nods. "She is. It's going to be a gorgeous event. Make sure to wear something formal." While she's walking away, she smiles at me over her shoulder. "You should bring your date."

"I agree," Adrienne says. "I'd like to officially meet him."

Dani winks. "Me too."

I shake my head. "He's not going to want to go to a wedding with me. Our relationship is still new. Inviting him to the wedding is like taking the next step."

"What's wrong with that?" Dani asks incredulously.

Adrienne places a hand on Dani's shoulder, gently

pushing her away. "D, let me handle this. You're not helping."

Dani throws her hands up in the air. "Fine, I'm done." She winks at me again and disappears into the pantry.

Adrienne laughs softly. "That girl is too much sometimes."

I nod. "That she is, but she's never afraid of anything. I wish I could be like that."

"You are, in your own way. As far as the wedding, there's nothing wrong with asking Kai to go as friends." Eyes narrowed, she studies me. "Although, I don't think that's really what you want."

Deep down, I know how I truly feel. I just don't want to move so fast, not like I did at the club. That was a mistake, one I don't want to make again. "It's not," I confess. "Kai is amazing and we've been spending a lot of time together."

"But, you haven't slept together, right?"

I shake my head. "Not yet. I want to more than anything, but I don't want to get hurt."

"That's a risk you have to take, Alex. You have to let people in. If you don't, you might end up with the wrong person. Getting hurt is going to happen. My heart has been broken more times than I can count, but if it weren't for those bad times, I wouldn't have found my husband. I'm glad I made all those mistakes." She squeezes my shoulders reassuringly. "You need to take a chance. You alone know what your heart is telling you. Listen to it."

As much as I want to protect myself, I have to stop running. Kai is a wonderful man and hasn't given me a reason not to trust him. "You know what, Adrienne, you're absolutely right. I know what I have to do."

Taking a deep breath, I pull out my phone and walk outside. The sky is blue with thin, white wisps of clouds floating by. It's the perfect day. I search for Kai's number and hit send.

"Hey, beautiful," he answers.

"Hi, how are you?"

"Great now that you've called. Is everything okay? I didn't think I'd hear from you until you got off from work."

I smile. "Everything's fine. There's something I want to ask you. You're more than welcome to say no. I know it's kind of last minute."

"What is it?"

Just the sound of his voice makes me shiver. I don't think I'll ever get tired of it. "There's a wedding this weekend and I was wondering if you wanted to go with me." The line goes silent and I start to panic. "If you're busy, that's totally fine. You don't have to go with me."

He bursts out laughing. "I'd be happy to be your date. At least, this way, people can actually see us together. It's time we made our relationship official."

Heart racing, I can't deny how amazing that sounds. "I couldn't have said it better."

THE WEEK FLIES by and I can't shake the butterflies in my stomach. When the doorbell rings, I hold my breath as I open the door. Kai stands there, all decked out in a tux with his hair gelled to perfection.

His eyes slide down my body. Since the wedding is formal, I didn't have much in my closet for it. I didn't want a long, formal gown, so I bought a short, midnight purple one with crystal beading around the waist.

"You look ..."

"It's the dress, I know. I fell in love with it, too," I say, joking around.

His eyes darken and it makes me tingle in all the right places. "That, and you're stunning in it."

Giggling, I lock the door behind me. "You don't look too bad yourself." Taking my hand, he leads me to his car and opens the door.

On the way there, he holds my hand, never once letting it go. "Thanks for inviting me tonight."

Glancing over at him, I smile. "Thanks for coming with me. My friends want to officially meet you."

"I look forward to it." It doesn't take long to get to the venue, and when we arrive, there are a ton of cars. Kai is pleased and grins wide. "We get to make a grand appearance it seems."

My nerves are shot. It's our first social event together and I know people will talk, but I'm ready for us to be out in the open. There's valet parking so Kai gets out and opens my door, taking my hand to help me out. Dani is in line to get inside, and when she sees us, she waves frantically and rushes to join us. Her long, green evening gown looks amazing with her skin and chocolate-colored hair.

"Hey, you two. I'm glad you're here. I didn't want to walk in by myself."

"You didn't have a date?" I ask.

She waves me off. "I was hoping to meet some single, handsome men. So far, it's looking like they're all taken." Grinning wide, she holds a hand out to Kai. "I'm Dani. We haven't officially met. I went to school with Alex."

Kai smiles and shakes her hand. "Kai Robicheau. Alex has told me a lot about you."

"Hopefully, all good stuff."

I wink. "Of course." Once inside the door, we sign our

names on the registry and find our seats. I glance around the room to see if I recognize anyone, but none stand out.

"Adrienne's not coming," Dani says sadly.

Finding some vacant seats, we sit down. "Why not?"

Sighing, she sits down beside me. "She wasn't feeling well. You saw how swollen her feet were before we left. I doubt she'll be working for much longer."

"That sucks. I wonder if Sandy's going to hire someone while she's out on maternity leave."

Dani shrugs. "Don't know. She probably needs to. Not unless she retires and shuts down."

A part of me wishes she would so I can branch out on my own like I've always wanted. Until then, I'm going to stay with Sandy. More people flood through the doors and there's not a vacant seat in the venue. The flowers are exquisite, all different shades of pink. It reminds me of Shelby's wedding in *Steel Magnolias*.

Kai squeezes my hand. "I don't think I've ever seen so much pink in my life."

I giggle. "True, but it's beautiful." It's then that I notice several of the attendees sneaking glances in our direction, mainly women. Leaning into him, I whisper in his ear, "You seem to be drawing some attention."

He shakes his head. "It's all you, love. All I can say is that it's going to be hard to keep my hands off of you tonight."

"Who says you have to?"

His eyes flash with need and I smile. "We're officially together now, right?"

"Yes," he answers, his voice low and dangerously sexy. "You're mine."

The groom and his groomsmen take up their places in the front and the music starts to play. We stand for the bride as she enters and I can't hold back the tears as Rayna and her newfound husband say their vows. Weddings always make me cry.

THE DINNER IS AMAZING, but it doesn't compare to Let's Get Baked. I can tell it by the expression on Sandy's face as she eats a piece of the rosemary chicken. Dani snickers. "She doesn't know how to hide it, does she?"

I laugh. "Nope."

"I have to agree," Kai says, finishing off the last of his roasted potatoes. "This doesn't compare to your cooking."

"Thanks," I reply sweetly. His hand slips under the table and I jump as he tickles the inside of my thigh.

Dani doesn't notice and nudges me in the side. "He's so cute. I love the way he looks at you."

I glance over at him and smile. "I do, too." My legs break out in chill bumps and he chuckles.

The bride and groom take the floor for their first dance and cameras flash all around. Once they're done, the DJ changes the song and everyone rushes out to dance. Dani gasps and points at a guy across the room. "Oh my God, is that Ben McCormick?"

I look at the guy closely and slap a hand over my mouth. "I think it is."

About that time, he notices her and walks toward our table, clearly recognizing us. "Dani? Alexandria?" he asks.

I wave. "Hi, Ben. It's good to see you."

"Likewise. You both look amazing." Then his focus lands on Dani. "Are you here with someone?"

Dani's grin widens. "Nope. You?"

He shakes his head. "Here by myself. Care to dance?"

"Sure." She takes his hand and they disappear onto the dance floor.

"Who is he?" Kai asks.

"Dani's old high school fling. They were together their junior and senior year, and broke up before he left for college."

Kai focuses on them dancing. "I'm just glad you and your ex didn't hit it off."

"Me too."

A slow dance plays over the speakers and a sly grin spreads across his face. It's "Kiss You Tonight" by David Nail. "Wanna dance?"

I bite my lip. "I'm not very good at it."

Chuckling, he stands and pulls me with him. "I highly doubt that."

On the dance floor, he's holding me so close that I can feel his heartbeat against my chest. His lips lightly touch my neck and my whole body trembles. "I want you tonight," I whisper.

A low growl rumbles in his chest, and he looks down at me, his eyes dark and raw. "You sure? I don't want you to feel pressured."

I shake my head. "You've never made me feel like that. I just hope I can last until we get to the house. Your teasing didn't help matters."

He quickly glances around the room and focuses in on the hallway. "Come with me."

Taking my hand, we walk off the dance floor and down the hallway. There are other doors, but I have no clue where they lead. Kai opens one of them and it appears to be the room where Rayna and her bridesmaids got dressed in.

"What are we doing?" I ask, glancing behind us.

Kai opens another door, and it's obvious it's where the

groom and his men prepared. There are beer bottles lined up on the dressing table and clothes everywhere. Kai pulls me inside and locks the door. "The groomsmen are too busy to come back here. We should have a few minutes."

Pulse racing, I'm both excited and yet scared of being caught. Kai picks me up and drops me on the leather love seat. "I want to taste you, Alex. And then once we're done in here, I want to take you home and make love to you."

I suck in a breath and he kisses me, pushing my lips open with his tongue. I want him so bad, I can barely breathe. Sliding his hand down the top of my dress, he squeezes my breast and lifts it out, not wasting any time in ravaging my nipple. I bite my lip to keep from screaming out. It all feels so damn good.

Kai settles between my legs and glides his hands up my thighs, taking my dress with him. Spreading my legs wider, I hold my breath, waiting for his lips to touch me.

TWENTY-THREE

Kai

———————

*A*lex tenses under my touch, giving me pause. She says she's ready, but I'm not one hundred percent sure at the moment. I don't want to scare her off or do something she doesn't like. It's not like we can sit down and fill out a questionnaire about what we like and don't like. I can see it now, *Do you like your clit sucked, bit, tugged, or all of the above?* Talk about making sex as impersonal as you can get.

I kiss my way up her thigh and nuzzle the outside of her pink panties, inhaling her scent. Her hips flex and I smile against her skin. Maybe she's nervous that we'll get caught and that this is what she really wants. I like the idea of teasing her though, so I move to her other thigh and make my way down her leg, nipping at her skin as I go along.

When I get to her leg, I pick it and pay special attention to the back of her knee. I either read or heard somewhere that this is an erogenous zone for women and this feels like the best time to test my limited knowledge. One lick and Alex's heel slams into my back.

Her eyes go wide and she covers her mouth. "Sorry," she

mumbles behind her hand. I chuckle and mentally add this spot for later exploration. I look at this woman, the one I have been fighting for, and smile. She squirms under my gaze, a sure sign that she's probably growing impatient with my stalling. Truthfully, so am I, but I'm jumpy. I'm afraid that I won't live up to her standards. It's a tall task to be someone's partner after they've been hurt by another.

Gently, I put one of her legs on the back of the couch and the other over my shoulder. Bending forward, my arm goes under her thigh and back over so my fingers can grip her panties. There isn't time for me to undress her, although the thought of taking her thong home is very appealing. My response to her arousal is automatic. My dick hardens knowing that I'm about to taste this woman for the first time. I keep my eyes focused on her as my tongue darts out and flicks her bud. Her hips buck and her fingers grip my hair. When she doesn't tell me to stop, I forge head and lick my tongue softly along the slit of her lips.

I peek at Alex to make sure she's still okay before turning my attention to her glistening pussy. Another lick elicits a moan and her hips buck. I delve my tongue inside, tasting her sweetness, and exploring every square inch of her. My thumb rubs her swollen clit until my mouth takes over, nipping and sucking on her bud. Alex thrashes around, muttering out a slew of favorable yesses and refers to me as God.

Alex gasps when I slip a finger inside of her. The heel of her foot pushes into my shoulder blade with each pump. "You're so fucking tight," I whisper against her skin. Thinking about being buried balls deep inside of her has my dick straining against my pants. I'm going to have to go rub one out before we return to the wedding.

Fuck, the wedding. I almost forgot, and am hoping that

no one is really missing her right now, although I sort of like the idea if they are. Alex's other leg drops to my shoulder as I continue to work her over with my tongue and finger. Softly, I push in a second and she tightens, until it's coated in her wetness and moving freely in and out of her core.

With my mouth on her clit and my fingers thrusting rapidly, her legs tighten around my head, holding me in place as her hips buck, fucking my face. She cries out and tries to muffle the rest of her noises. I want to tell her that tonight she can scream as loud as she wants, that I want everyone to know and hear that her boyfriend is fucking her.

"I'm gonna come ... oh my God, I'm gonna ..."

Her words have me moving faster. I want to watch her, to see her face as she unleashes her essence all over my fingers, but I don't want to stop. The jab of her heels into my back and the rigid pulling of my hair is a sure sign that she's about to explode.

I pull back slightly and rub her clit vigorously, pumping my fingers inside of her warmth. She all but flies off the couch when her walls start contracting, making me wish it were my dick that was inside of her. I slow down and ride out the wave of euphoria until I pull my hand away from her and stick my fingers in my mouth to taste her again.

Alex lies there with her legs haphazardly placed around me, her panties sort of on her but not, and her beautiful dress pushed up over her hips. Leaning forward, I kiss her deeply, letting her taste herself off my lips. She pulls me down, in between her legs, and starts to grind against me.

"Not here, babe." It's agonizing to tell her that, but I don't want our first time be in the dressing room at some fancy wedding. Reluctantly, I sit back and try to adjust without hurting myself.

"Are you sure? I could ..." Her eyes fall to my dick, which is pitching a circus size tent.

I shake my head. "Tonight," I murmur as my thumb strokes her cheek. "Let's get you back out there before your friends start to wonder."

Alex nods and stands up. She fixes herself rather easily and checks her reflection in the mirror. Thank God for hairspray because her hair looks flawless—not that I'd find anything wrong with her ever.

We walk out of the room, as if we had taken a wrong turn. There are only a few people in the hallway and none of them seem suspicious. When I see the sign for the bathroom, I pull Alex close. "I need to go take care of my problem."

"I could've helped," she says into my ear as her hand ghosts over the front of my pants, making my dick jump.

Holding back a groan, I bite her shoulder. "Baby, I want to fuck you so bad right now, but if my dick sees you, it's game over."

Alex fucking giggles and it kills me. "How long will you be?"

I step back and look at my very hard dick. "Seconds at this rate."

"I'll meet you at the table." She kisses me softly and sashays away. Thankfully she doesn't look back before disappearing into the ballroom. Fortunately for me, the bathroom is empty. I pick the stall at the end and lock myself in, thankful for the floor to ceiling walls.

I groan as soon as my hand wraps around my dick. It doesn't take much for me to imagine that I'm with Alex as I start to stroke my cock. I've never timed myself when it comes to jacking off, but I'm willing to bet this is a record. I'm half of a dozen rubs in when my balls tighten. Somehow, I'm able to grab a fistful of toilet paper before I come all over the place.

Each grunt is met with hip action and a spurt into the wad of paper. It's ridiculous that my body thinks that I'm actually fucking someone, aside from air. It's almost like my hips needed to move in order to expel the contents.

I clean up as quickly as I can and return to the reception. It doesn't take me long to spot Alex, who isn't at our table, but standing off to the side, chatting with her friend Dani. Coming up behind her, I place my hand on her hip and kiss her shoulder.

"Would you like to dance?" I ask her, hoping that she'll say yes. Looking at me from over her shoulder, Alex nods. She gives her hand and I lead her out and onto the floor. She feels good in my arms, like she was meant to be here. This wedding was a turning point for us. I don't know if it's because weddings are emotional and can bring out the best and worst in people, or because she's ready. Either way, I don't care. I have her in my arms and there isn't any other place I'd rather be.

Our foreheads rest against each other's, both of us knowing that the dynamic in our relationship has shifted, and for the better. No, I don't want to say things are better. They're different and it's that good kind of different people embrace.

"I know you said you can't dance, but I can. All you have to do is relax and let me move your body. Do you trust me?"

"Yes," she replies, as her fingers play with the back of my hair.

She trusts me. I swallow the lump in my throat. It couldn't have been easy for her say yes, knowing that she's been hurt in the past. The fact that she trusts me—whether it's with dancing or being intimate with her when anyone could've walked in on us—means everything to me. I guess patience and perseverance really does pay off.

The song switches and I guide her into the middle of the dance floor. Other women stare at her as I twirl her around and command her body to do things she never knew she was capable of. Alex laughs, she apologizes profusely when she steps on my toes, she tumbles, and she glides like a princess fairy across the dance floor.

When I dip her, I take advantage of her elongated neck and exposed skin, and I kiss her softly, working my way up her body as I pull her up until our eyes meet and our lips finally connect. We kiss throughout the remainder of the song, parting only when someone booms into the microphone that it's time for the bouquet toss.

I leave her standing in the middle of the floor as her friend from work comes rushing toward her. At the bar, I grab a drink and watch as the gaggle of women crowd together.

"Hey, man. Sorry, but I forgot your name," the man next to me says as he shakes my hand.

"Kai. You're Dani's ex, right?"

"Yeah, Ben McCormick. So have you and Alex been dating long?"

I shake my head. "A couple of weeks," I tell him. "We met at a function my boss was having. She was catering it."

Ben laughs. "Man, she used to cook for all of us in home economics class. We would scramble to find out which hour she had it just so we could eat her food."

"I don't blame you. Alex can cook. It's a good thing I have a gym membership."

"I hear that."

Ben and I cease talking when the bouquet flies through

the air. I'm straining to see if my girl catches, but the crowd is too thick. I see an arm raised, but can't tell if it's Alex or not.

When she bursts through the crowd, the beaming smile on her face tells all. I don't even notice the arrangement hanging by her side.

"Looks like you're next, buddy." Ben slaps me on the shoulder and takes off after Dani.

"Well will you look at that," I say, as I pull her close to me.

"I out jumped them all."

"Maybe this calls for a little celebration?"

"What'd you have in mind?" she asks.

I lean and whisper into her ear, "My bed and you screaming my name?"

Alex flushes. Pulling her lower lip in between her teeth, she nods. We leave without saying good-bye. No need to alert anyone because it will only lead to questions.

TWENTY-FOUR

Alexandria

*T*he ride to Kai's house is agonizing. I don't know what's come over me. Yeah, I was a little nervous letting him go down on me at a wedding, but it's like it unleashed a whole new me. For the first time in my life, I feel spontaneous and free. It's a good feeling.

"Why are you smiling like that?" Kai asks.

I tear my gaze away from the window and my thoughts and smile at him. "Just thinking."

"About what?" Reaching over, he slides a hand up my thigh. It was only about an hour ago he had those fingers of his inside of me.

Heat rises to my cheeks. "You. I can't help but be nervous about tonight."

"Why is that?"

Shrugging, I focus back on the road. It's dark and the city lights blur as we pass by. "I'm not exactly experienced with men. You can count the number I've been with on one hand."

His fingers grasp my chin. "Hey, look at me." We pull

up to a stoplight and I look into his eyes. "We can take it slow tonight, if you want. It might not be a bad idea to."

I can't help but snicker. "Worked up, are you?"

He chuckles. "You know I am. I've never had to jack off in a public restroom before, much less a wedding. But it was fun."

"If you don't last long tonight, you can make it up to me in the morning," I say with a wink.

His eyes widen. "Does that mean you're staying the entire night?"

"We'll see. I don't have any extra clothes with me though."

He squeezes my thigh. "You can wear some of mine."

I know it sounds crazy, but I've always wanted to wake up in a man's shirt after a long night of love making. I always saw it happen in the movies. Maybe it's the hopeless romantic in me. Picking up the pace, Kai speeds down the highway and it doesn't take long to get to his apartment. I've been to his place so much the past couple of weeks, it's become a second home. When we get inside, I shiver from the cold. Kai rubs his hands down my arms to warm me, but it doesn't work.

"Looks like we need to get in bed so I can warm you up," he teases, kissing the side of my neck.

More shivers rake down my body. "Maybe so."

I squeal as he picks me up in his arms and carries me to his room. I love his room because it smells just like him. The comforter on his king size bed is a charcoal gray that also matches the color of the walls. It's very sexy and masculine.

"You sure this is what you want? There's no turning back once we do this," he murmurs in my ear.

I shake my head. "I'm more than ready. I just want to be with you."

A low growl rumbles in his chest and it makes everything inside of me tighten. He sets me down and turns me toward him. Cupping my cheeks, he stares deep into my eyes and rests his forehead to mine. "I believe I'm falling in love with you, Alex. All I ever think about is you and of the next moment we're going to be together." I try to pull back, but he holds me tighter. "I'm not trying to scare you."

"You're not," I murmur, placing my hands over his. "I love you, too, Kai."

Groaning, his eyes darken with raw, primal need. "That's all I wanted to hear." He moves closer and puts his fingers underneath my chin, lifting gently. "There are so many things I want to do to you right now."

He trails his hands down my shoulders and over the skin of my back until he reaches the zipper to my dress. "Like what?" I ask breathlessly.

Unzipping my dress, he lets if fall to the floor with a mischievous smirk on his face. "Like how I'm going to make your body scream for my touch ... and how I'm going enjoy making you come in every way possible."

Eyes wide, I don't have time to speak before he closes his lips over mine, silencing me. My clit throbs in anticipation, aching for release. I want him ... need him. In one swift move, he lifts me up in his arms and I straddle his waist, holding on tight as we fall on the bed.

Covering me with his body, he spreads my legs with his knee. I still have on my strapless pink bra and pink thong, but Kai's gaze is focused solely on mine as he kisses me, claims me. He rocks his body against mine, lifting my left leg around his waist so he can press his cock harder between my legs.

The momentum builds to the point I can't contain the

silence any more. "Kai," I gasp, my chest rising and falling rapidly.

Digging my nails into his arm, he knows I'm about to come. Quickly, he slides his hand down my thigh to the inside of it, and finally over my thong, rubbing my clit with his thumb.

I'm not fully there yet, but as soon as he slides his fingers inside of me it's all over. My body tightens and I scream out my pleasure, grasping onto his arms and squeezing until the tingling subsides, leaving me breathless and aching for more. Lifting his fingers to his lips, Kai puts them in his mouth and closes his eyes, moaning as he tastes me on them.

Ripping off my underwear, he throws it across the room before lifting me up in his arms so he can unlatch my bra. Roughly, he kisses me and I can't help but moan when he throws my bra off to the side and pinches my nipples. He bites my lip and sucks it hard, making a strangled cry escape my lips as he massages and squeezes my breasts.

I'm in heaven.

I've never felt this level of intensity with anyone before, not even my mystery man at the club.

I can't wait any longer to have him inside of me, so I grasp the button on his pants and open them.

Chuckling, Kai slides off the bed and lowers his pants and boxer briefs to the floor. "Is this what you want?" he asks. "I figured you'd want to take things slow."

"No," I moan breathlessly. "If you make me wait any longer, I'm going to go insane."

As soon as I get a good look at his body, I visibly tremble, which earns another chuckle to escape his lips. He towers over me on the bed, and spreads my legs wide so he can rest between them. Reaching toward the dresser, he opens the top drawer, pulls out a condom, and expertly slides it down his long, thick cock.

"I guess I can't leave you waiting then." Smirking, he lowers his lips to my breasts and flicks one of my nipples with his tongue. I gasp and arch my back, waiting on him to do it again. This time, when he closes his lips over me, he bites and sucks hard while massaging me with his strong hands.

Groaning, he opens my legs wider and pushes his cock in just an inch; it's enough to get me panting. *More*, I want to scream.

As if he hears my silent plea, he rocks his hips and slides in farther ... and farther until he's fully inside of me, filling me. It hurts like hell—the burn making me clench and grit my teeth to keep from crying out—but it's a pleasurable pain. Slowly, Kai moves along to a silent rhythm and holds me tight, alternating those lips of his to each one of my breasts, suckling and nipping them with his teeth.

"You feel and taste so damn good," he growls, moving his lips to my neck. Holding my face in his hands, he brings his mouth to mine and thrusts his tongue inside, claiming me in every way he possibly could.

He picks up his pace and thrusts harder inside of me, lifting my legs and wrapping them around his waist; I gasp when I feel him go deeper. Instead of pulling out and pushing back in with long strokes, he stays deep and rocks his hips hard, keeping a continual rhythm against my clit.

"Oh my God," I cry, closing my eyes. "Please keep doing that."

His low growl vibrates in my ear, and I can feel him getting harder inside of me. He's close and so am I. Squeezing him harder with my legs, I hold on tight and bite *his* lip this time, feeling his cock pulsate.

"If you keep clenching down on me, baby, I'm not going to last."

I'm not going to last either. Rocking my hips, I let my orgasm send me over the edge, crying out when Kai digs his fingers in my back as he, too, releases inside of me. Slick with sweat, his muscles tense and flex beneath my hands as I hold onto him, silently waiting on the pain to hit when he pulls out.

"Are you okay? I could see it in your eyes that it hurt you in the beginning." Gently, he pulls out and rolls over to his side so he can slide the condom off and throw it away before holding me in his arms.

"It hurt," I admit nervously, "but I figured it would once I got a good look at you."

He smiles, but then it disappears. "When was the last time you've been with a man?"

Sadly, I look into his eyes and sigh. "A while. I've only been with one other man."

His eyes widen. "If I'd known that, I wouldn't have gone so hard."

"It's okay, I promise."

Brushing the hair off my face, he holds onto my chin and kisses my lips. "Stay here, I'll be right back. I know what'll help you."

Sliding off the bed, he hurries into the bathroom and shuts the door. Water begins to run and I can hear him moving around. A few minutes later, the door opens and I expect the light to blind me, but it doesn't. There's a soft glow coming from inside.

I start to get up, but Kai stops me by lifting me up into his arms. "I got you, baby," he murmurs.

"I can walk you know," I tease as he carries me into the bathroom.

The room is lit with candlelight, and the bathtub—big enough to fit ten people—is surrounded by dozens of them, and steamy from the hot, bubbly water.

"It smells amazing." The scent reminds me of chamomile and lavender.

After setting me in the water, he climbs in behind me. I immediately relax when he puts his arms around me. I lay my head against his chest and breathe him in, trembling as he runs his warm hands over my heated skin.

There's nothing sexual about the way he's caressing my arms and my back, but my insides clench and light up like fire. I want him again. My body is sore, but I need more.

The bathtub is filled almost to the brim with water, so I slowly turn around to face him, straddling his waist. Furrowing his brows, he gazes down at my lips, and then back up to my eyes.

"Are you okay? Do you want to get out?" I shake my head and reached down into the water, wrapping my hand around his cock. Immediately, it jumps and hardens. Kai moans and leans his head against the tub. "Are you sure this is what you want? I don't want to hurt you."

The harder his cock gets, the harder I massage him. "I'm not worried about that. Just sit back and let me do the work this time."

Holding his face in my hand, I kiss his lips and plunge my tongue inside so I can taste him. I moan into his mouth and slide my body against him, holding him close. My clit throbs uncontrollably, and I know I won't last long once I get started, even if it does hurt.

"Do we need to use a—"

"No," I growl, biting his earlobe. "I'm on the pill. Guess I should've told you that earlier."

Moaning, he lifts me up in his arms and tilts me back so he can suck my nipples. "Then what are you waiting for?"

I lower onto his body and slide all the way down. The soothing water helps the tenderness, but I can still feel him stretching me. It feels so amazingly good I don't want it to end.

TWENTY-FIVE

Kai

*P*ortland is worth it. My projects are booming and Parker is praising me every time I see him. Things with Alex ... they're fucking amazing. I thought for sure the initial "newness" of our relationship would start to trickle, become mundane. I was wrong. I can't wait to get off work every day to rush home to her. She's either at my place or I'm at hers. We've swapped keys. Given each other space in our closets. And have even started finishing each other's sentences.

I knew from the moment that I saw Alex she was meant for me. It was something that I felt deeply the moment our eyes met. After our initial meeting, I almost didn't call her, but something told me not to give up, and I am thankful that I listened to that nagging voice in the back of my head.

I finish my workout and head for the shower. If I'm lucky, Alex will still be sleeping when I get back to my apartment and I can crawl in with her for a few more minutes before she has to leave for work. The days of me checking out the females at the gym have long passed. Not a single one interests me. None of them compare to Alex. It's totally cliché for me to say this, but I hit the jackpot when she came into my life.

Opening the door, I'm relieved to find that the lights are still off. Alex is snuggled around my pillow, sleeping softly. I slip off my sweats and pull my shirt off so I can climb back into bed with her.

"Hmm, you smell good," she says as she replaces the pillow with my chest. Having her in my arms is the daily jolt I need to function. "How was the gym?"

"I don't know, you tell me," I say as I take her hand and trail it down my abs. She trails her hand farther and cups me on the outside of my boxers.

"Babe," I warn. She has about five minutes before she has to be up for work, and while I'd love to indulge in morning sex, the thought of getting her in trouble with Sandy is not high on my priority list.

Her hand stills and she sighs. "Raincheck?"

I turn, pushing her on her side. Her lips are soft against mine as I kiss her. "Of course. I think you know I'll cash in." I lean down to kiss her again, but her phone rings. She reaches over and answers it.

"Hey, Mom ... no, I'm getting ready for work ... okay ... okay ... I'll let you know."

Alex hangs up and turns off her alarm before it can ring out. "That was my mom," she says, although I already know that. "So I told her about you and she'd like for you to come to dinner ... tonight." She glances at me only briefly.

I raise her chin so she's looking into my eyes. "Do you want me to meet your parents?"

She shrugs. "My dad ... he's not the easiest to get along with. We don't exactly see eye to eye. He's very old fashioned and hasn't agreed with any of the decisions I've made in my life."

"So I should probably keep things PG and not ask you to suck me off in your childhood bedroom?" I laugh. Alex's eyes go wide and she shakes her head frantically. "I wouldn't, babe. But I'd love to meet your parents. Should I meet you there? Or do you want to drive together?"

I know she's from Sweet Briar, but we rarely talk about her parents. Alex has hinted a few times that she doesn't get along with her father, so I have never pressed her for more information. Now I'm going to meet him tonight, and I hope that things go well. Not just for my sake, but Alex's as well. Taking your boyfriend home to meet your parents is never an easy thing. Believe me I know. My mom won't stop hounding me about Alex and when I'm bringing her to Arizona. The problem is, I'm so busy at work, and I can't find the time to take off. Right now, my free time focuses around Alex and sometimes she has to work on the weekends. On those nights, I wait for her to come home.

I can't seem to get enough of Alex, and the thought of sharing her with my mother for a weekend doesn't seem like something I want to do right now, except if I meet hers, she needs to meet mine.

"I'll meet you there," she says. "No use in you having to drive back."

Cupping her cheek, I press my lips to hers. "You know I'll come back and pick you up. Besides, I think I'd like to show you around the job site. And what if after dinner you have some built up tension that I need to fuck out of you?"

Alex laughs. "You drive a hard bargain, Mr. Robicheau. I'll tell Sandy that I need to leave early today, we're only prepping for tomorrow."

"Perfect."

Unfortunately, Alex has to leave my bed. I watch as her

pert ass sashays to my bathroom. This woman is going to kill me.

PASTOR LARRY AND MAYOR STAN find me inside one of our finished stores while I'm meeting with the new tenants. We're all excited that they'll be moving in and after a few modifications to the interior they'll start installing their products next week.

The two men of the town linger near the storefront. Honestly, it's a bit annoying as they shouldn't be here or they should at least wait outside, but both of them take the revitalization project seriously, although for different reasons. Larry wants to see his town thrive. He wants people to move back here and start their families. I can understand where Larry is coming from, but Stan, he wants the popularity coming with the project. We've caught a reporter's attention and he comes out here once a week to check on the progress. Of course, Stan is front and center, telling the reporter and the people watching everything that is going on. Most of the time he's wrong and Ward Enterprises has to issue a press release correcting Stan. Parker has spoken to him a few times about keeping his nose out of our business, but the pleas have fallen on deaf ears.

Glancing down at my phone, I realize the time. I need to leave now in order to get Alex and come back for dinner with her parents. That is something I'm not willing to be late for. The last thing I want to do is give her father an excuse to say something to her.

As I finish up with my client, Larry and Stan meander over to me, as if we have some business to discuss. I try to ignore them, but it's near impossible.

It's Stan who slams his hand onto my shoulder, jostling me forward. "Do you think they're the best fit?" he asks.

I look at him squarely and shake my head. "I'm not sure I follow." I continue to put the contract and drawings back into my bag.

"Well, they sell ..." Stan pauses and looks around before leaning into my ear. "Lingerie."

I laugh. They do in fact sell lingerie. I even ordered some as a gift for Alex. "They sell clothing, Stan. Surely, your wife wears bras?"

His face pales and he stumbles for words. I shake my head and nod toward Larry as I grab my bag. "If you'll excuse me, gentleman. I have another appointment." I wait for them by the door, impatiently I might add.

"Kai, I'm having a dinner party tonight. I'd like to invite you."

"Thank you, but I have a prior engagement."

Larry nods. "Well, if you finish in a timely manner, stop by. My daughter will be there, and like I've said before, I'd like to introduce you. I think you'd be good for her."

"I appreciate that Larry, but I have a girlfriend," I tell him. It's the same thing I've been telling him before Alex and I even got together.

Again, Stan's hand falls onto my shoulder. "Nothing wrong with playing the field."

Shaking my head, I push open the door so the men will leave. "Have a good night and enjoy your party, Larry." I don't bother saying anything to Stan as I get into my car. I can't stand the man. He's a pompous ass who is all about taking credit for other's hard work. I don't have time in my life for people like that.

Thankfully, the drive to Alex's is done with little traffic, and by the time I reach her house, my temper has calmed. I can't imagine spending the evening with the likes of Stan. Even if I didn't have Alex, I would tell Larry no for the simple fact that mayor will be there.

When I walk in, all I hear is Alex singing. She's not the best singer, but can carry a tune and I don't mind listening to her, especially when she's shaking her cute little butt to the music. I find her in the bathroom, putting on make-up.

"You're gorgeous without it, ya know."

She smiles at me through the mirror. "Thank you, but sometimes—"

"Don't," I say as my hand rests on her hip. "Don't sell yourself short because your father is an ass. You're the most beautiful woman I know and I'm crazy in love with you." I kiss her bare shoulder and then her neck. Her ear is next until she turns and crashes her lips to mine. She tastes fucking divine. "I've missed you all day," I tell her as I pull away. If I don't, I'll have her legs wrapped around my waist and we'll be going at on her bathroom counter.

"Let's skip dinner," she says, kissing a path down my neck. "You can eat me instead."

Let me introduce you to horny Alex. *This* is not the same woman I met months ago. No, this is the one that let loose after the first time we slept together. I told her there wasn't a thing she could say or do to me that would turn me off ... unless she was breaking up with me. I teased her a bit the first few times and would ask her what she wanted and would only give it to her once she expressed herself. Now, it's automatic, and I love it.

"As much as I would love to bury my face between your legs, this is an important step for us. My parents want to meet you. We just have to find a weekend that you're not working and we'll go."

Alex's head falls to my shoulder. I feel bad for forcing

the issue, but the last thing I want is for her parents to think I don't want meet them. I do. I plan to be a part of Alex's life for a long time and want her parents to like me. I know it's stupid of me to say that I see a future with her, but I do. Everything with her is so easy. It's like we've been together for years, minus the split living situation, which I'd like to change soon.

TWENTY-SIX

Alexandria

"Who's going to be at the dinner?" Kai asks.

We're almost to my parents' house and I'm dreading it. It's been months since I've seen or talked to my father. "Let's see, Sandy will be there so I'm excited about that. My parents' neighbors and friends, and whoever else wants to be there will be there. Growing up, they had dinners at the house all the time, but I always invited my friends."

Reaching over, Kai takes my hand. "You have me this time."

I just hope and pray my parents love him like I do. It doesn't matter if they do or not, but it will be nice if they do. We pull up to the light blue, perfect house I grew up in and there are cars lined up and down the street.

We park down the street and walk hand in hand up to the house. "This is where you grew up?"

I nod. "It is, and I'm going to apologize in advance for whatever happens in there."

His brows furrow. "Is your dad really that bad?"

My eyes burn. "No. Growing up, we used to do so

much together. Then, when I started high school, it's like I was in prison. I wasn't allowed to do anything my friends were doing. That's why I couldn't wait to go to college."

Kai squeezes my hand. "You have an overprotective father. I'm sure his actions were because he loves you. You can damn well bet I'll be the same way if we ever have a daughter."

The thought makes me smile. "You said *we*."

A sly grin spreads across his face. "Who knows."

I can just imagine a little girl with dark hair and his bright blue eyes. We walk inside and my mother is talking to Sandy. Her eyes widen when she sees us. Instead of sliding around on her scooter, she limps over to us.

"You came. I'm so happy." She pulls me into her arms and I hug her tight. "He's handsome," she says, whispering in my ear.

Giggling, I let her go. There's a twinkle in her eyes as she looks at Kai. "Mom, this is Kai Robicheau." I look up at Kai. "Kai, this is my mom, Regina Miller."

Kai shakes her hand. "Thank you for inviting me. It's nice to meet you."

"Same, my dear. Hopefully, you and Alexandria will come around more often. I miss seeing my little girl."

"That depends all on Dad," I grumble low so only my mother can hear.

She sighs. "He's excited to see you."

"Where is he?" I ask.

"Not sure," she replies, glancing around the room. "Maybe in the kitchen."

"I'll find him in a little bit."

My mother cups my cheek and smiles. "Be nice. You'll be surprised how much he's changed." Then she grins up at

Kai. "I'm going to check on the food. We should be good to eat very soon."

She walks off and Kai chuckles. "You look just like her."

"So I've been told." Taking his hand, I pull him through the living room.

"Kai, over here buddy," someone calls out.

Kai stops and glances over his shoulder and then back to me. "It's Stan. I can't stand the bastard."

Stan walks over, his beady eyes on me like he's checking me out.

"I can see why," I whisper for only him to hear.

"Who's your date?" Stan asks.

Kai's jaw clenches, but he smiles. "Stan, this is my girlfriend, Alex."

Stan holds out his hand. "You are very beautiful, Alex. How'd you get mixed up with this guy?"

Grinning wide, I shake his hand. "I got lucky." I look up at Kai and nod toward Sandy who's in the corner, talking to Dani's mother, Brenda. "I'll be right back."

Kai nods and I walk away. Sandy waves frantically at me and I hurry over. "Your mother told me you were coming. There's so much I want to tell you. I was just discussing it with Dani's mother."

Brenda gives me a hug. "You'll love it. I'll let you two talk in private."

Excitement bubbles in my chest. "What's going on?"

She takes in a deep breath. "I finally decided it's time to retire. I thought about giving the business to you and Dani."

"Seriously?" I squeal.

She bursts out laughing. "Yes, but for a small fee. I know owning your own place is something you've wanted for a long time. You and Dani would be amazing partners."

"What about Adrienne?"

"Once the baby comes, she's decided to stay home. Dani doesn't know yet. I wanted to tell you first."

Flinging my arms around her neck, I squeeze her tight. "Thank you so much. I don't know what to say."

"Say you'll accept."

"Yes," I gasp, letting her go. "I'd be more than happy to."

"Good. I'll contact my lawyer and get the papers drawn up."

"Sounds perfect to me." My dreams are finally coming true. I want to tell Kai the good news, but I don't see him anywhere. I start toward the kitchen and my dad walks out, freezing when he gets a good look at me. His gray hair is still short, combed over on the top like he's always worn it ever since before I was born. I expect to see disappointment on his face, but there's a smile instead, only it's sad.

He opens his arms and closes the distance. "Lexi. It's so good to see you, darling."

I hug him back. "Hey, Dad."

Placing his hands on my shoulders, he pulls me back and smiles. "I saw you talking to Sandy. Did she tell you the good news?"

I nodded happily. "She did. I'm so excited I can barely think straight."

"When she told us, I knew you'd be happy. It's been your dream for a long time."

"Yes, it has," I mention sadly. I've never really taken the time to talk to my father about the things I wanted out of life, not since I yelled them at him before I left for college. It was the first time I had the guts to express how I felt.

His eyes water and it makes mine burn. "I've missed you, Lexi. Over the last few months, I kept hoping you'd come see me."

"It works both ways, Dad."

He nods once and drops his gaze. "I know. I can't turn back time, but we can go forward. Sometimes it's hard to face the fact that I'm old and that you're not a little girl anymore. I wanted to hold onto that for as long as I could."

His words break my heart. "It's okay. I know you were hard and strict because you love me."

"I do, sweetheart. More than you'll ever know." He smiles again and gasps. "Oh, I have someone for you to meet."

"Who is it?" I ask.

"A man I know. I think he'll be a good match for you."

Putting his arm around me, he leads me toward the kitchen, but I stop. "Dad, no, I can't. I'm with someone now."

His brows furrow. "Oh yeah?"

At that time, Kai appears in the doorway, mouth gaping as he looks from me to my father. "Yes," I say nervously, pointing at Kai. "He's right there."

My father peers over at Kai and wide grin spreads across his face. "Well, look what we got here."

Kai walks over, seeming unsure. "Did I miss something?"

My father extends his hand and Kai shakes it. "Obviously, we all did. You didn't tell me you were dating my daughter."

"Wait," I gasp, staring curiously at them both, "how do you two know each other?"

Chuckling, my father nods at Kai. "I've been working with this young man on the Sweet Briar project. I gave him your number a while back. I'm glad to see you two finally met." My father kisses me on the head. "I'll be right back."

As soon as he walks off, I cross my arms over my chest. "He gave you my number, huh?"

Laughing, Kai shakes his head. "Who would've thought it'd be you."

I wrap my arms around his neck. "Why didn't you call?"

He holds me tight. "I think Stan took it from me. It doesn't matter now, we're together. The coincidence is uncanny."

"Some would say it's fate, but I don't know if I believe in that stuff."

His lips connect with mine and I melt into him. "Either way, you're mine now."

"Yes, I am."

THE DINNER WENT great and my parents absolutely love Kai, so do the women from the church. My parents made us promise to visit them every other Sunday afternoon after my father's done with his church sermons. It's late by the time we arrive back at Kai's apartment. My eyes are heavy and all I want to do is sleep.

Kai opens the door and he follows me into the bedroom. Laying down on the bed, I breathe in the smell of him on the sheets. "Has the excitement worn you out?" he asks with a laugh.

Grinning from ear to ear, I hold his pillow to my chest. "You have no idea. Everything's falling into place just the way I want it."

He lies down beside me. "I know. You and Dani have a lot of talking to do when you go back to work."

"I can't believe I'm going to be part owner of Let's Get Baked. I don't have to start from scratch."

"No, you don't. I'm here if you need help."

I place my hand on top of his. "I know you are. You have no idea how much I appreciate that."

He kisses my hand. "I understand now why you and your father didn't get along when you were growing up. He's a preacher who wanted his daughter to keep her innocence."

"Yeah," I agree. "I feel so guilty for avoiding him. I just didn't want to hear him preach to me about what I'm doing wrong in this world."

"Did he do that tonight?"

A tear falls down the side of my face. "No, that's what makes my heart ache. By avoiding him, I've hurt him. The sadness in his eyes is something I don't ever want to see again."

"You won't have to," he murmurs. "I think we made him happy tonight. Not to mention, your parents conned us into visiting them every other weekend."

I burst out laughing. "Yes, they did."

Kai grabs my waist and slides me into his body. "I'm starting to get used to this."

Snuggling into his arms, I breathe him in. "Me too." I close my eyes and I can feel my mind drifting away.

"I love you, Alex."

I smile. "And I love you."

TWENTY-SEVEN

Kai

*T*oday is the day that I officially ask Alex to move in with me. We're going furniture shopping under the guise that I need a new dining room table. The one I have now is small, and completely covered with the plans for Let's Get Baked. It would be nice to say that my girl is a business owner, but Dani didn't have her share of the deposit, which held up the closing. I was tempted to buy Sandy out and hand the business over to Alex, but I knew that Alex had worked hard to save the money and I wanted her to feel successful.

Still, that hasn't stopped Alex and Dani from drawing up new plans for the kitchen. I hovered until my opinion was asked. Sometimes they took it, other times I would get up in the middle of the night and make the subtle changes I knew their contractor would make regardless.

Since she took me home to meet her parents, she's stayed at my apartment each night. It would make sense for us to move to her house, but it's small with only one-bedroom, and it can fit in my place. I love that she's here, but definitely want to her to make this her home until we can buy a house together.

Buying a house and putting down roots isn't something I've ever thought about. Even when I was living in Malibu, renting was the only option for me. Buying means commitment, and until now I wasn't interested in getting that far in life.

Alex and I walk hand in hand through the furniture store. I have seen a few tables I like, but I'm waiting for Alex to have that ah ha moment, and then I'll ask her. I'm nervous and I'm surprised she hasn't noticed that I'm fidgeting or that my palm is sweating. I don't know why it's such a big deal. It's not like I'm asking her to marry me.

We test out each option. By test, Alex sits down, she measures, and stands back to look at every angle while I put all my weight on the wood to make sure it can withstand the pressure ... you know for when we christen it. I have my priorities.

"What do you think about this one?" she asks. Her face is pinched as she peers at the table. "It can seat four until you have company and it will expand to eight."

"We," I say, correcting her.

"Huh?"

"You said, 'when I have company' and I corrected you. It's when 'we' have company."

Alex brushes me off. "It's your place, Kai."

I move toward her. "Why don't we make it our place?"

Narrowing her eyes, she tilts her head.

"Alexandria Miller, I know we haven't been dating long, but I would like to know if you'd like to move in with me?"

"Kai—"

"Say yes," yells the lady behind Alex. I nod, giving her a silent thank you.

"Think about it, babe. You haven't spent a single night at your place since you took me home to meet your parents. You're paying rent and utilities for a place you're not using, plus you're about to open your own business. You're going to be busy and the last thing I want is to put pressure on you after you've had a long day, but you know it's going to happen. You know I'm going to ask you to come over or I'll be at your place and you'll feel like you need to entertain me. If we're living in one place, we're home and together. We won't feel pressured when we have to work late. You won't stress about your house and the bills that come with it."

"You'll charge me rent, right? I'll be allowed to pay my half?"

"Of course, babe. Fifty-fifty all the way, except for this table. I'll buy that because it's needed, unless you want to take the spare bedroom and make it an office for the both of us. We can ditch the table and buy a few desks and book-shelves."

"What about when your parents come to visit?"

"They won't. My mom doesn't fly and I she definitely won't drive this far. Right now, it's storage. I'll gladly share the room with you."

Alex ponders my proposal, and by the expression on her face she's going to say yes. When she nods rapidly, I pull her into my arms and kiss her. The people lingering around start clapping, which honestly is a bit embarrassing. I set her back down and kiss her again.

"Let's go look at other furniture."

"Wait," she says, halting me. "The table ... I sort of really like it."

Grinning widely, I search for a sales person. "We'll take this, but we'll be adding some more."

Alex and I rush to the other section and start looking at desks and the configuration we could make. The shitty part is that I don't have the dimension of the room so it'll be rather hard for us to buy anything tonight, but we can get a good idea of what we want and come back another night.

We head back toward the sales desk with a good idea of what we want, and that is when I have that moment, the one you never want to have in front of the woman you're in love with.

I try to hide my face, but eye contact was already made. When Jenica realizes it's me, her eyes light up. Seriously? This woman knows my most sordid details and she's excited to see me. And fuck my life, she's coming toward us. How the hell am I going to explain to Alex that I was paying for sex?

"Hi, Kai!"

"Jenica," I say curtly. I'm definitely not interested in introducing her to Alex.

"You know, I heard about this happening, but haven't witnessed it until now."

"What is that exactly?" I ask. I can feel Alex's eyes on me, but there is no way in hell that I'll look at her.

"You guys! I mean, how did figure it out? Did you break the rules?"

Closing my eyes, I swallow hard. I'm having a hard time processing what Jenica is saying. I don't want to assume, but it sounds like Alex was my partner at the club, and that just can't be.

"Um ... where do you work?" the soft voice of Alex asks.

"Society X. I was Kai's escort. Jared's yours, right?"

My head starts to spin as I step away from Alex. I can't even comprehend what I'm hearing right now.

"Oh shit, I didn't know that you didn't know ... wow,

what a coincidence that you would hook up outside of the club."

I want to puke. If I'm assuming right, I took Alex's virginity in the dark room. I don't even care about the other shit we did because what took place in the dark room is bigger than all that.

I finally have the courage to look at Alex, who is pale. I don't know if I should reach out to her or what. The high from today is gone. It no longer exists.

"Are you ready to pay for the table?"

I shake my head and turn toward the exit, leaving Alex in the showroom. I can't wrap my head around the fact that she used the club to lose her virginity.

The more I think about it, the angrier I become. When Alex steps out, she doesn't look at me. I don't know where we go from here, but right now I can't be with her. Pulling my keys out of my pocket, I toss them at her. "You can take my car. I need some time to think."

"Kai?" she says, her voice low and hollow.

I stop, but keep my back to her. "Don't, Alex. What you did ..." I can't finish my sentence without insulting her and that's not what I want to do. Something possessed her to use the club, and while I shouldn't judge because I was there too, the fact remains she gave a complete stranger something that she should've held sacred to her. That is what kills me.

I haven't a clue as to where I'm going. I'm just walking. It's getting dark and I'm hungry, but I can't fathom eating anything right now. I finally happen along the train station. I pay my fee and wait for the next one to arrive. There are couples all around me, each one making more jealous because up until a few hours ago, I had that.

And now I don't know what I have besides a broken heart and a very confused brain. I know I need to talk to her, but I don't know what to say. I need to know why she did that and how many other men she was with ...

That's when the second or third shock of the night hits. I replay our first Saturday date in my mind. I had texted Jenica the night before, hoping to go back into the room with my partner. This was after Alex told me she was seeing someone and didn't want to get involved with me, except she was already involved with me.

I went to the room, but Alex wasn't there. Some other woman was and I walked out. That night, Alex was upset. She was upset because of me, without even knowing it.

"What a fucking mess," I say out loud.

"You can say that again," the man next to me mutters. I don't know about his day, but mine has turned out to be pretty fucking shitty.

The train ride takes me two hours until I'm somewhat near my place. I'm thankful for the warmer weather, but this walking shit is for the birds. But there was no way I could be in the car with her, stuck in traffic, and not explode. I know myself better than that.

Of course, my apartment is empty when I get there. My car keys are on the counter, but everything that was Alex's is gone. I'm not surprised, but hate that she chose the flight option instead of staying to fight for us. Me, I had to walk away. I guess she did, too.

In the dark, I stare at the wall with my phone in my hand. Her name is on my screen, waiting for me to press the button. When I finally do, it rings three times before her pained voice answers.

"Why, Alex? Please tell me why you decided to lose your virginity in the club?"

TWENTY-EIGHT

Alexandria

"*W*hy Alex? Please tell me why you decided to lose your virginity in the club?"

I'm so embarrassed, pissed, and ashamed all at once, I can't even begin to tell him why. "I can't explain it over the phone. Come to my house and we can talk. That is, if you want to."

The phone goes silent but then his heavy sigh echoes through the phone. "I'll be right there."

I hang up without saying good-bye. My eyes feel like sandpaper from crying so much. With the way Kai reacted to everything, it left me so confused I don't know what to think. He's angry, I get it, but so am I. Leaving me the way he did hurt more than knowing the truth.

Heart racing, I pace the living room floor. It was Kai this whole time. The man I messed around with in the play room and even lost my virginity to is the man I'm in love with. What are the odds of those two men being one in the same?

Nerves shot, I hurry into the kitchen and bypass the wine straight to the liquor. I'm not a hardcore drinker, but I need it tonight. The first vodka shot goes down with a slight burn, but the second is just like water as it slides smooth down my throat. I toss back a third and can already feel the muscles in my body ease. The sound of Kai's car rumbles in the driveway, so I grab the bottle of vodka and sit on the couch, propping my feet up on the coffee table. The front door opens and I can't even bring myself to look at him.

After shutting the door lightly, he walks into the living room. The tension in the air skyrockets. "Are you drunk?"

As much as I want to take another swig of vodka, I set the bottle down on the table. "Not yet, but I'm feeling pretty good at the moment."

Instead of sitting beside me, he chooses the recliner across from me. "You never answered my question."

"You mean the one about me losing my virginity in the club?" It's in this moment I finally look in his eyes. I want to break down and collapse into his arms, and pretend none of this ever happened, but I can't.

"Why?" he asks, voice shaking.

I throw my hands up in the air. "Hell, I don't know. A part of me was intrigued with the whole idea when Dani told me about the club. You know who my father is. The guys in school stayed away from me, and by the time college came around, I was too focused on my classes to even get intimate with a guy. The club gave me a way to express myself and try things I've never done before."

His brows furrow. "You never went down on a guy before until me?"

I shake my head. "And I've never let a guy go down on me before either."

"How did you even know what to do if you hadn't done it before?"

Huffing, I roll my eyes. "There is such a thing as porno

movies, Kai. I may be a preacher's daughter, but I'm also human. I wanted to experience it all."

"How many other men were you with at the club?" His eyes darken and I snap.

"Seriously, you're going to ask me that? What about you? You're not the only one who got hurt." He stares at me for a few seconds and then looks away. "*You* are the only one I was ever with. And *you* are the one who stood me up that last night in the dark room."

His head snaps up. "I showed up. I was there. Hell, I'm the one who set it up so why the fuck would I stand you up? When I went into the room it everything was wrong. The way the woman was tied to the table and her body. I knew that wasn't you. Before I even went in I knew I wasn't going to do what you had requested because I'm not into spankings and I could pretty guess you weren't either. I was pissed. I ripped into Jenica and told I was done." My heart stops. He was in the play room while I was in the dark room. It only makes me angrier with Society X for screwing up. "You're the only woman I was ever with there, Alex. I never wanted to sign up in the first place. My co-worker, Bryant ... my first day at Ward Enterprises we head out to visit Sweet Briar. He says he wants to take me to lunch and since I'm new, of course I'm going to go. But we end up at that place and I drove, so it's not like I can tell him to catch a ride back to the office. I met Jenica and she gave me a tour. I wasn't interested, so I filled out the application with these ridiculous fetishes because in my mind I'm never stepping foot in there again.

"Then I get call or text. I don't remember how it all started, but I'm new in town and working a ton of hours and since I had been in the club I was having these urges, and I have this message that some random chick wants to give me head. So I went."

Hands shaking, he clasps them together and lowers his head. "When I took your virginity, that was the hardest thing I've ever done. A part of me wanted to walk out of the room, but I couldn't." Tears flood down my cheeks and I bite my lip to keep from crying out. "From the beginning, we had a connection, Alex. All I wanted was to be with you, but I couldn't help but wonder what made you want to give away something so precious to someone at a sex club. Did you ever consider how that would've made me feel?"

I scoff and glare at him. "We were in a sex club remember? Feelings weren't supposed to matter. I didn't think you'd care."

He stares right at me. "I did, Alex. I'm not the kind of guy who gets off on taking advantage of someone. I might not have known who you were at the time, but I cared about you. It was real to me. It was important to me. And it scared the fuck out of me because I couldn't wrap my head around why someone would want to do that? That is supposed to be sacred and ... it's supposed to be shared with someone you love or even like, someone you know. I wasn't raised to take advantage of women. I get that we were in a sex club, but ... my feelings mattered, Alex. That night, everything mattered."

"And what are we now? We're pissed at each other for things we had no control over. I think I'm more embarrassed and ashamed than anything. But I have to say, when you found out it was me, you ran away and left me to pick up the pieces. *That* is something I can't get over."

With a heavy sigh, Kai kneels down in front of me. I can see the sorrow and regret on his face, but it still doesn't change the fact that he left in a fit of rage. It makes me wonder if he'll always be like that.

"I'm sorry, Alex. I wish you knew how bad you brain-fucked me that night in the dark room. I wanted you so bad, and the whole time we were making love, I was afraid I was hurting you. It felt wrong. The whole time I wanted to talk to you. I wanted to look into your eyes and thank you for trusting me with your body, but I couldn't. We couldn't be the way we should've been because of their fucked up rules. I wanted to give you my number, anything so I could see you outside that place.

"And when Jenica was standing there, saying that shit to us, my mind was reeling. I'm not pissed at you ... or us. I'm upset because this situation is beyond fucked up, Alex. What are the chances? Portland is a big city and here we are, in love, and we find out our relationship started in a sex club. I find out the woman I'm in love with, who cut out on a date early, was doing so, so she could go be with me? And said woman gave me her virginity? That's some fucked up shit, Alex, and I'm sorry if I reacted wrong, but I've never been in a situation like this."

"But it was me," I cry. "And when you found out the truth, I could see the horror on your face and you walked away from me. Do you even care how that made *me* feel?" He tries to hold my hands, but I move them away and stand, putting as much distance between us as I can. "I think we've said enough for the night."

"What are we going to do now, Alex?" he murmurs.

I shrug. "I don't know, but I think we should let everything process for a few days. My heart hurts too much right now."

The room grows silent, but I can see his reflection in the glass cabinet I have in the living room. Eyes red, he looks just as distressed as me. He steps closer and reaches out a hand, but then pulls it back. "I love you, Alexandria. Running away was wrong and I should've stayed to make sure you were okay. I was a coward and acting irrationally. I can't ... I needed help understanding why ... Please say you can forgive me."

"You're forgiven," I whisper, glancing at him over my shoulder. "But I need you to leave."

Deep down, I don't want him to leave, but so much has happened. I need time to think. With a single nod, Kai turns on his heel and walks out the door, shutting it gently behind him. I thought my heart hurt before, but hearing him speed away split it right in two.

"HOLY SHIT, so it was Kai the whole time?" Dani shrieks.

I drop the dumplings into the pot and nod. "And when he found out, he tossed his car keys at me and left. It was the worst feeling ever."

Holding out her arms, Dani closes the distance and hugs me, dusting me with flour in the process. "I can imagine. Do you want me to kick his ass?"

"No," I laugh. "We'll figure out everything soon. It's only been a day."

I look around the kitchen and smile. One day soon it's going to be mine and Dani's. For now, it's still Sandy's, and we have clients to cook for. Adrienne has decided to spend the last of her pregnancy at home so she can rest.

Dani pats my back and lets me go. "A day can feel like ten years sometimes."

I snort. "Got that right."

"Has he tried to call you?"

"I don't know. I turned my phone off. I'm not ready to face him again. I feel so stupid."

A sad expression crosses her face. "And I'm partway to blame for that. If it wasn't for me, you never would've gone to that club. I thought you were having fun there."

Flashbacks of my nights there appear in my mind. I can't help but smile. "I was," I reply honestly. "I did a lot of things I never thought I'd do. It helped me find the real me."

"For that, I'm glad. You're not little miss goody-goody two shoes anymore."

I wink, trying my best to smile. "Deep down, I never was."

She runs a hand down my arm. "You both will work it out. I have no doubt. He loves you too much to walk away over something stupid. I mean, you two were basically cheating on each other with each other. Sounds crazy just thinking about it."

"It does," I agree. My heart still hurts each time it beats. "All I want is for things to get back to normal."

"They will, girlie. And I think I know how to help you with that."

"Oh yeah?"

Her grin widens. "I'm going to the bank today to apply for a business loan. That way, we can get this place up and running like we want."

True excitement fills my chest and I squeal. With the way things are with Kai, I need the distraction.

TWENTY-NINE

Kai

I have never called in sick, and yet for the last two days I have because I haven't felt like leaving my room. I have never felt this way, like I was dying. It's the only way to explain how my body aches right now. Every bone hurts. Breathing is painful. My heart ... well, I'm not even sure that's beating right now. Also, I couldn't face Larry and the people of Sweet Briar, pretending everything is okay. They love Alex and I don't think I have a decent poker face to play it off. They'd see right through me, and know instantly that something has happened.

And what do I say to her father when he asks why I'm on the outs with his daughter? "Sorry, Larry, but it seems that your daughter and I were having a bit of fun in these rooms at a sex club and I took her virginity. But hey, the best part is that I didn't know her name or know what she looked like because everything is meant to be anonymous."

Yeah, something tells me that Larry and I will no longer be friends, and I don't even want to think about what he'd say to Alex. This whole situation is fucked up, and the worst part is that I don't have Alex to help me figure it out.

I overreacted. There is no other way to say it. My brain took over and my heart died a little. Not only from my decision to walk away from Alex, but because I had been bothered by the fact that I took a woman's virginity in a sex club. To find out it was Alex ... I don't know, I never expected her to be someone who needed to do that, but then again, I'm not someone who seeks out attention in that way. We both made choices we have to live with, and I was wrong to treat her like hers were bad.

When she told me that she needed me to leave the other night, I almost refused. I wanted to pull her into my arms and show her how much I love her. Truth be told, I wanted to pick her up and carry her to her room and make love to her as if it were our very first time again. But she wouldn't have it. Not that I blame her.

I think the only thing saving me from going crazy is the knowledge that I'm the only one she's been with. I don't know what I'd do if there were more. It's stupid to even think that since I've been with other women, but this club ... I don't know, it makes you think differently.

Every twenty to thirty minutes, I call Alex, only to have her phone go to voicemail. I'd give anything to go back and change my reaction. Actually, I'd rip into Jenica for violating our privacy. What if it wasn't Alex I'd been with and Jenica said something? She could've ruined what Alex and I are building. I thought the whole point of Society X was to be discreet.

Thinking this has me looking up the number to the club. There is no way I want to talk to Jenica, but they need to know the damage they've caused. My thumb hovers over the phone number, waiting to be pressed. "Fuck it," I say out loud.

"Society X," the female voice answers.

"Hi, yes. I'd like to speak with the manager."

"Is there a problem that I can help with, sir?"

"I need to report one of the employees for violating my privacy."

"One moment, sir." The woman puts me on hold without asking me any more questions. I get the sense that they take this type of stuff seriously.

"This is Bryce."

"Are you the person I'd file a complaint with?" I ask.

The man laughs. "I'm the owner," he says.

"Perfect. I am, or was a member of your club, but after a colossal mix up on one of my requests I decided not to come back. I also entered into a serious relationship, which brings me to my complaint. The other day, my girlfriend and I ran into Jenica, who proceeds to carry on about how my girlfriend was my partner in the rooms I was using. Bryce, neither of us knew this. It's not a question I tend to ask women that I'm with if they're frequenting your establishment, nor would I expect them to ask me. Needless to say, your employee has violated our confidentiality agreements and I'm rather upset."

"I must ask, did you violate our rules?" he asks, as if his employee could do no wrong.

"Neither of us did, and frankly, I didn't even want to be there. Thing is, my co-worker brought me there for lunch and Jenica wouldn't take no for an answer. Now that I think about it, I'm sure she works on commission and probably has some quota that has to be met." I finish by telling him about my application process and how I lied.

He sighs heavily. "I'll refund your fee and give you and your girlfriend free access to the club for a year."

I roll my eyes. Does he really think Alex and I will be back? "And that's our only recourse? Free membership?"

"Certainly not. You can sue the club, but you have to prove her disclosing this information caused you harm."

I think about what he says for a minute. The only harm is if Alex and I can't get over this hump and end up breaking up. Short of telling him that I want Jenica fired, I don't have much recourse.

"Personally, I think I've had enough of the club. Jenica's lack of attention to detail has really ruined it for me, not to mention the humiliation my girlfriend and I experienced when Jenica blurted out our private details in a store."

I hang up, not giving him a chance to respond. The complaint may be filed, but I don't feel any better about it. However, at least he knows that his employees can't be trusted. It won't fix things between Alex and I either, but it's something.

Lying in my bed, I know I have to do something. Alex won't take my calls, and yet she's upset because I walked away. So what exactly is she doing? I crawl out of bed and head for the shower. Her shampoo is still in there and I find myself smelling the contents instead of washing. But as it happens, ideas start coming to me on how I'm going to win her back. She's the only reason I'm willing to stay in Portland. If she doesn't want me, I'm going to finish the Sweet Briar project and cut my losses.

IT PAYS TO HAVE CONNECTIONS. I briefly explained to Parker what was going on. I left out the club part, telling him that I made a mistake and have to make amends. The only way to do that is to find out where Alex is working today. Thankfully, he has Sandy's number and gave it to me.

Sandy was very eager to help, giving me the address to where Alex and Dani were working. When she told me it was a baby shower, I thought I was stupid for even thinking about showing up there, but I'm a desperate man who wants his girlfriend back in his arms.

With my arms full of flowers and chocolates, I enter the venue where the girls are working. Women squeal and start clapping, until someone blurts out that I'm not the mother-to-be's husband. I wink at all of them as I make my way toward Alex who is standing there with a ladle in her hand and her mouth hanging wide open.

Setting the flowers and candies down, I cup her cheeks between my hands and kiss her. I don't care that her mouth is open or that she can beat me over my head with the large spoon. I kiss her because I've missed the hell out of her these past two days and she needs to know it.

"Kai," she says my name with a tone that dates back to our first outing. I should take note and step away, cut my losses, but she's too damn important to me to give up.

"These are for you," I say, handing her the five-dozen roses I picked up. I look around for the pregnant woman and rush the box of chocolates to her.

"Sorry for the interruption, but you see, I love that woman more than anything. I think maybe I was in love with her the first time I saw her, and I really need her to forgive me."

"What'd you do?" she asks.

I look back at Alex whose eyes go wide. Smiling, I turn back toward the guest of honor. "Rushed to judgment. Typical man thing, right, ladies?"

There's a chorus of yeses, each making me feel about two feet tall.

"Do you love him?" someone yells out. I glance back at Alex, who looks at the woman and then me.

"I do."

"Sweetie, don't waste love on feeling the hate. Go after your man." I want to hug, kiss, and twirl that woman around to show her my gratitude, but my attention is trained right on Alex. She sets her serving spoon down and takes cautious steps toward me. Dani is there, watching this all play out. She leans into Alex and whispers something in her ear.

It's like everything moves in slow motion. Even the voices around sound distorted. Each step that Alex takes toward me, there seems to one step going in a different direction. She's running at me or it's a fast walk considering we're only a few feet from each other.

I catch her in my arms and crash my lips against hers. We're spinning slowly and everyone around us is clapping. This has to be one of the best feelings in the world. I say one of because if I have my way, Alex and I are going to have many more to come.

She slides down my body. Her cheeks are flushed and I know I've embarrassed her. Wrapping her in my arms, I shield her from the onlookers. "I love you, Alex. These past few days have been the worst I have ever experienced. I'm sorry for being a jerk and I promise you that it'll happen again."

Alex pulls back and looks at me. "What?"

"Oh, babe, you heard me. I'm going to mess up. I'm going to be an ass. I'll come home moody, work late nights and forget things. I'll leave dishes in the sink, dirty socks on the floor, and forget about the toilet seat. But the one thing that will never change is that I'm madly in love with you."

"Shit, if she doesn't marry him, I will," someone says.

Alex smiles. Yeah, that's coming next ... I'm not sure when but I have every intention of asking her to marry me. I don't care if we haven't been together long. Being without her is not something I ever want to be.

"I love you, too."

"Now, will you move in with me? I miss having all your stuff everywhere. Your side of the bed is cold and your scent is gone. I need it, Alexandria. I need you."

"Say yes!" they all yell.

"Alex, if you don't, I will," Dani adds.

"It seems that either I move in or you'll have a harem of women living with you."

I smile down at her. "There's only one woman for me, and that's you." Our lips meet much to the delight of everyone in the room. It's hard to smile while kissing her, but I am. This is good practice for when we get married, and I make a mental note to get everyone's names so we can invite them.

THIRTY

Alexandria

*T*oday is the big day. Dani's and mine renovations have been done on the kitchen and Let's Get Baked is officially ours. It's a dream come true. Dani and I worked all night to prepare our favorite foods for our guests. The place smells heavenly, but I'm too nervous to eat.

I look out the window and the parking lot is filled with people, waiting for us to cut the ribbon. My parents are there along with their friends from the church. However, my main focus is on all the news station vans and cameras. Kai said he was going to make sure it was the biggest event in Portland on this sunny Saturday morning and he was absolutely right.

"I can't believe this is happening," Dani whispers, coming up beside me. She peeks out the window and smiles. "Thank you for being patient with me. I didn't expect this to happen so fast. I don't know how to thank Kai for helping us as much as he has."

I slide my arm around her shoulders. "You've already thanked him a gazillion times." Glancing outside, I blow out a nervous breath. "It's a little overwhelming, especially with that crowd, isn't it?"

She snickers. "Just a little. If this exposure brings in a shit ton more people, we'll have to hire more workers."

"That's a good problem to have."

Dani nudges me in the arm. "Hey, aren't you officially moving in with Kai tomorrow?"

My heart flutters as I watch him through the window. "Yep. Everything is packed up and ready to go. My house will be on the market in a few days."

"What does your dad say about that? I know he's against people moving in with each other before marriage."

I shrug. "He is, but he's finally got it through his head that I'm an adult and I can make my own decisions. Besides, he loves Kai to death. They get along great."

"That's good. Maybe one day I'll find someone like Kai."

"There's a lot of single, handsome men at Ward Enterprises. I can see if Kai can introduce you to some."

She snorts. "Hell yeah. I'm down for that."

"Good, I'll see what he can do." More people pull into the parking lot. "We should probably get out there."

She nods nervously. "Okay, let's do this."

We walk out the back door and around to the front where everyone waits on us. Cameras flash and I wave, hoping like hell I don't appear as nervous as I feel. Kai waves us over to a woman in a red business suit with long, blonde hair, holding a microphone. I recognize her from one of the TV stations.

Reaching for my hand, Kai pulls me closer. "Alex, this is Samantha Crane with WVTV Channel 3. They're going to report live as they walk through the kitchen."

I shake Samantha's hand. "It's a pleasure to meet you. Dani and I are happy you're here."

Samantha's eyes twinkle. "Me too. I keep hearing wonderful things about your place. I'm excited to eat some of the food."

"There's a ton of it," Dani laughs. "Alex's miniature quiches are the best."

"So are Dani's apple pies," Kai adds. "They're amazing."

Dani blushes and I can't help but smile. Kai hands me the scissors and I turn to Dani. "Ready to cut the ribbon?"

Her eyes glisten. "If you are."

We walk over to the ribbon and face the crowd. Everyone goes silent. I look out at the crowd and wave. "Thank you, everyone, for coming out to see us on this special day. Dani and I are super excited to venture on this amazing journey together. We're thankful and extremely grateful to be able to share this day with you."

Holding the scissors in my hand, Dani places hers on top of mine. "Here we go," I whisper.

We cut the ribbon and the crowd whistles and shouts for joy. Dani steps to the other side of the walkway and we greet everyone as they walk inside. Once everyone enters, Dani joins while I stand in the doorway with Kai. Grinning wide, he glances around the kitchen. "Your parents are so proud of you," he murmurs. "You should've heard your father talking about you."

I look over at my parents who are busy tasting the food. "It feels good to be close to them again. I'm glad I finally made him proud."

He slides his arm around my waist. "He was always proud of you, Alex. I know I am. You've worked so hard getting this place ready." He turns me to face him. "If you're tired tomorrow, we can postpone moving your stuff into my apartment."

Wrapping my arms around his neck, I squeeze him hard. "Nothing is going to keep me from moving in with you."

His lips pull back in a sly grin. "Good, because we have a lot of celebrating to do."

"I THINK that's the last of it," Kai says, hauling in the last two boxes.

His living room is filled with boxes, not to mention, the kitchen. It's fully stocked now that I have all of my appliances in there. The kitchen is my domain. I have everything set where I want it.

Kai sets the boxes down on the floor, and then flops down on the couch. "Want to know one of the things I'm going to like with you being here every night?" he calls out.

I glance over at him from the kitchen, but I can only see the back of his head. "What is that?"

He winks back at me. "I don't ever have to cook or clean again. I have you to do it for me."

"Oh no you didn't." Grabbing my empty bottle of water, I throw it at his head. He dodges it and bursts out laughing. I know he's kidding. "I am not here to be your maid, asshole."

His smile slowly transforms to a sly grin as he makes his way into the kitchen. Gaze narrowed, I step away and he follows me. "Why are you looking at me like that?"

He shrugs, continuing to stalk me as my heart races and excitement rushes through my veins. I love it when he stares at me with those raw, passion-filled eyes of his. It makes everything inside of me tighten in anticipation.

"Instead of a maid, you could always be my sex slave. How does that sound?"

"Sounds pretty kinky, Mr. Robicheau. Didn't think you were still into the Society X stuff."

His eyes darken. "This has nothing to do with that place. Now that you're here, we can do whatever we want together and when we want it."

I bite my lip. "What do you have in mind?"

Closing the distance, he picks me up in his arms. "It's time to officially christen this place as ours. I want to make love to you in our bed, in the kitchen, on the floor, and even on the dining room table." He licks his lips. "I bet some chocolate syrup would taste fucking incredible on your skin."

This time, I lick my lips. I'd love to drizzle some chocolate on his. "What are we waiting for?"

He carries me into the bedroom and sets me down, but he doesn't let me out of his arms.

Nuzzling my neck, he pushes my hair out of the way so he can kiss his way up my jaw. Tilting my head to the side, I moan and close my eyes. Chill bumps race across my skin and I shiver, leaning against him to steal some of his warmth. He chuckles in my ear and presses his hard cock against my stomach, lightly thrusting it up and down. I hold him tight.

"I want more," I breathe.

The words spark the need inside of him. Kissing me feverishly, he picks me up in his arms and gently sets me on the bed.

"I'm going to give you more, baby. Don't worry," he promises. Sliding his fingers under my shirt, he lifts it up over my head and throws it on the floor. He moans deep in his chest when he gazes down at me with his sexy blue eyes, licking his lips. Kissing the mounds of my breasts, he lowers the fabric over one and begins to suck on my taut, sensitive nipple while reaching behind me to unclasp my bra. He shoves it away, still keeping his lips enclosed over my breast. I want to feel him inside of me, to satiate the craving between my legs.

Already, my body responds to his touch and I'm achingly wet, so close to letting go. Fumbling with his jeans, I try desperately to get them undone so I can wrap my fingers around his cock and feel it pulsate with my touch. Kai helps me out, kicking off his jeans when I finally have them undone. Once he's free, I take him in my hands and squeeze, pumping him up and down.

"Fuck, that feels good," he groans. "Don't stop."

Harder and faster I stroke his length, enjoying the satisfied rumble in his chest. His fingers deftly unbutton my shorts and he slides them down my legs. With his arm around my waist, he moves up the bed and spreads my legs wide with his knee. Keeping his gaze on mine, he kisses me gently at first and then harder as he pushes his fingers inside of me. Gasping from the sensations, I open wider for him, loving the sound of his satisfied moans.

"Harder, Kai," I beg, spreading my legs wider.

He does as I ask, and as soon as he does it's my undoing. Tightening around his fingers, he bites down on my lip and sucks as I cry out in pleasure, riding the waves of my orgasm. Slowly, he rubs my sensitive clit with his thumb and swirls his fingers in the wetness between my legs. Keeping his gaze on mine, he traces my nipples with my desire, leaving wet trails in his wake, and sucks them both greedily. My body craves him. I can feel his cock pressing closer to my opening, and as soon as he pushes in just a tiny bit, I gasp.

"I love the noises you make. It's so fucking hot," he growls low.

Almost instantly, he pushes inside of me ... hard. Not only do I gasp, I cry out so loud I can barely recognize the sound of my own voice. Wrapping my legs around his waist, I rock my hips along with his and hold on tight, crying out with each thrust. The muscles in his back tighten and flex as he works his body into mine. I rake my nails down his back to his ass, loving the way it hardens with each thrust.

I'm so close to losing it again, my body clenching tight around his cock.

My breaths start coming out as pants as the ache between my legs gets stronger, wilder. We're both so close, and the moment I tip over the edge I dig my nails into his back just as he grips onto me tighter, plunging in as deep as he can and filling me with his release. Breathing hard, he takes my face in his hands.

"We made love on the bed. I think it's time we move to the shower. Then afterwards, the kitchen table." He slides a hand down my cheek to my breasts. "That way we'll be clean for the chocolate."

"You were serious about that?"

His eyes twinkle. "Oh yeah, baby. After I lick it off your entire body, we can get back in the water. I know shower sex is your favorite."

He's right, it is. There's something about hot, running water cascading all over my body and having him inside of me that turns me on like never before. I press my lips to his, nipping him with my teeth. "I'm ready."

THIRTY-ONE

Epilogue

---

*T*he sun is barely up as I walk the grounds of the newly built apartment complex. In a few short hours, this area will be bustling with news reporters, community members, Ward Enterprises, and new families moving into their brand new, energy efficient homes. Children will play on the jungle gyms, teenagers will swim in the pool, and the thousands of volunteers will carry boxes up as many as four flights of stairs to help people move in, while I'm sure Stan the mayor stands by and directs people on what to do.

I had hoped over the past eighteen months that he would slowly slip away, but unfortunately, he has been nothing but a thorn in my side and I don't see him going away anytime soon. I try to put myself in his shoes, but I can't. His vision of self-importance leaves something to be desired.

This revitalization project went a lot faster than I thought. I expected two years, if not two and a half to finish the apartments, but the crew was determined. Not only did they receive a hefty bonus from Parker, but also, I think with Dani and Alex coming around a few times a week with a buffet of food helped them work a lot faster. I may have threatened to cut them off with the food supply a time or two.

One thing that the Sweet Briar project has done was bring Alex and I a lot closer. Through her stories, I have been able to really bring Sweet Briar back to life. With the help of Parker, we contacted all the business owners in the "downtown" portion of town and remodeled, fixed, or repainted all the existing buildings to look similar. The conformity really makes the town look "old fashioned" but modern. Plus, it brings everyone up to code.

Once the cosmetic stuff was done, tourism started picking up. With the strip mall at capacity, the stores started seeing an increase in daily visitors. The city council began organizing events to draw more people to town. The sand castle building competition was intense, and I got to be one of the judges. Alex also saw this as an opportunity and purchased a food truck, which operates on the weekends near the newly constructed boardwalk. And Parker is currently in talks to develop a hotel along the beach.

It's easy to see why people love Sweet Briar now that I've spent a considerable amount of time here. I'm tempted to ask Alex if she wants to buy a house here, but I think she enjoys the distance that we have with her parents. We visit them on Sundays for dinner, and while Alex and Larry have a better relationship, there are still moments when they frustrate each other.

Now that the Sweet Briar project is over, Alex and I are flying to Arizona so she can finally meet my parents. It's been a long time coming, and while I could've easily taken her for a weekend, it wouldn't be enough for my mother.

She and Alex already spend hours on Sunday mornings talking or video chatting.

Wiping the morning dew off the swing, I sit down. My feet stay planted to the ground while I sway back and forth. Every project that I have worked on has meant something, but this one ... for some reason this means more. It's not a high-rise or some conglomerate building that will house Fortune 500 companies. This place will become someone's home, their place to hang their hat and build memories. If it weren't for Parker Ward, none of this would be feasible.

If it weren't for Parker, I wouldn't be here right now. I wouldn't be in love with Alex or thinking about our future together. We talk about marriage. We both know we want to get married, but with her starting a business, which was fairly successful when she took it over and now has tripled in volume, and my dedication to this project, we haven't made any definite plans. Not that plans need to be made. I just have to get down on bended knee and ask her. I've already asked Larry, or I should say that Larry has given me permission too many times to count. Alex says it's because he loves me. I tease her it's because he wants to get rid of her.

The slamming of doors breaks my reverie. I'm assuming it's the news crews that are here, along with the community members who are coming to witness the ribbon cutting cere- mony. I wasn't going to do one, but Alex was insistent. She said that it's like reaching the top of a mountain that you've been climbing for years and that when you get to the peak, everyone is there, waiting for you. I had set one up for her and Dani when they took over Let's Get Baked, but did so for the publicity. One of the things they changed was opening a shop. Not only do they cater, but they sell baked goods as well. I learned early on in our relationship that I have to pick and choose the arguments I want to pursue. Alex is evil and will withhold sex ... and by sex I mean food. My girl can cook, and if weren't for my gym membership and the fact that she loves sex I'd be buying bigger pants.

By the time I reach the main parking lot, hordes of people are gathering around. When I arrived first thing this morning I roped off the entrance with a massive ribbon, preventing people from entering. The renters have seen their places, but no one else. Parker and I didn't feel it was right.

Larry greets me with a smile as we come into view of each other. He's been a Godsend with all the projects and worked tirelessly to raise funds for extras. Instead of shaking hands, we hug. He pats me on the back.

"I can't thank you enough," he says when he pulls away. There are unshed tears in his eyes, causing me to choke up as well.

"I didn't do anything," I tell him. "It was all you and Parker." I'm always quick to point out that this project wasn't my doing. I only designed the concept and saw the implantation of it.

"You did a lot, Kai. More than you give yourself credit for."

I take his compliment to heart, wondering if some of it pertains to Alex as well. He often comments that she's changed since we've been together, and I like to think it's been for the better. I know she's made me a better man. In fact, I think she's perfect, and each night when I lie next to her I thank everything for her. I almost lost her, which now seems like the most trivial thing ever. But, man, I'm happy that she's given me her all, including the one thing that nearly destroyed us.

"There's a lot of people here," Larry points out. I look

out over the crowd in time to see Alex and Dani's food truck pull up, except Alex isn't in it because she's walking toward me, dressed like she's about to go church.

"Hey, babe," I say, pulling her to me so I can kiss her cheek. I like to keep things chaste in front of her parents. She whispers, "Good morning," in my ear before turning to face her dad.

"Morning, Dad. Dani has quiches in the truck if you're hungry. Is Mom coming?"

"Yes, she'll be here," he says. Larry kisses Alex on the cheek and rushes over to the truck.

"If I didn't know better, I'd think you're trying to steal my thunder." I nod toward the truck as Alex shakes her head.

Stepping closer, she straightens my tie. "I missed you this morning."

"Sorry. I couldn't sleep."

"Are you nervous?"

I shrug. "It's not nerves, but I don't know what it is. More excitement I think because people get to start moving in today."

"Everyone is going to love it," she tells me.

I kiss her quickly and take her hand in mine to lead her to the other side of the ribbon. Parker and his wife, Mia, are making their way through the crowd, as well as Bryant and his wife. Yes, she's the one he met at the club and started dating. There was a time when he started questioning his relationship, mostly because of how they met, and I thought about telling him about Alex and I but didn't. Bryant can be a little rough around the edges and I didn't want it getting back to Alex or Bryant saying something that would embarrass her.

Parker and Mia approach with a large pair of scissors in

her hand. She's excited as she greets Alex. "Well done, Kai. I suppose now isn't the time to ask you to sign another contract?" Parker asks as he shakes my hand.

When I first started, I thought I'd move on after this project, but once I met Alex Portland quickly became my home. "Considering I'm thinking of purchasing a house here, I better sign quickly." I laugh, hoping that he catches my drift.

He shakes his head. "Let's forget about a contract and make you a full-time employee at Ward Enterprises. I think Director of the Community Development Division with a full staff at your disposal might do the trick?"

"With a raise," Mia yells out at her husband.

Parker laughs. "After I've seen what you've done here, I'll pay you anything to stay on."

"Deal," I tell him as we shake hands.

"Great, now let's get this ribbon cut so people can move in," he says. Parker's presence is commanding. The second he shouts that we're about to start everyone moves into position. Mia hands the scissors to me, and while I'd love to be the one to cut the ribbon, it's not for me to do. I seek out Larry and beckon him forward.

"Without you, Sweet Briar would be one of those towns that people drive by," I say him as I hand him the tool. "I think you should do the honors."

Larry's smile beams as bright as the sun as he takes the scissors from me. He steps forward, but not before looking at Regina, Alex, me, and finally out to the people who have gathered. "Here goes everything," he says as he snips the ribbon. There's loud cheer and people surge forward to explore the grounds. Standing back, I watch as children run toward the playground, and one in particular hops onto the swing I sat in earlier.

"You did good," Alex whispers into my ear as she holds me from behind.

I hold on her arms and shake my head. "I didn't do anything, Alex. The people, they wanted this. I just gave them the guidance to succeed and Parker gave them the funds. Your dad ..." I pause and spread my arms out. "He did this. He knew what Sweet Briar needed and made it happen."

Alex nestles into me as we watch our surroundings. Trucks are starting to arrive and the community is getting ready to help unload belongings. It's going to be an all-day affair, and thanks to Let's Get Baked, everyone will be well fed.

"Follow me, there's someplace I want to take you." With Alex's hand in mine, we walk toward downtown. It's a couple-mile walk but the morning is beautiful and I honestly need this time to think. Alex must be enjoying the peace and quiet, too, because she hasn't said much since we left.

We finally make it to the beach where we trudge along in the sand until we're almost in sight of what I want to show her.

"Turn around and look."

She does. "What am I looking at?"

"That house." The house in question is in shambles.

"Hmm, okay?"

"The asking price is very low. It comes with two hundred feet of beach access. It would be a full gut job, but we could make it ours. It's three bedrooms with an attic that we can turn into another room or an office."

Alex turns and looks at me. "What are you saying, Kai?"

"I'm saying ... well, asking if you think we should buy that house? Do you want to invest with me and commit to remodeling our first home together? Take something and make it our own?" Turning, I face the ocean. "The master bedroom faces this view, Alex. We could wake up to this sound every day, and during the summer we could sleep with the doors open so we can hear the crashing of the waves." I glance at her, wondering what she's thinking. "What do you say, babe?"

"One condition," she says.

"Anything."

"Marry me," she blurts the words out. "I know I'm supposed to wait for you to ask, but that rule is dumb. I asked your mom—"

"You asked my mom?"

She nods. "I figured if you were going to ask me, you'd ask my dad, so I thought I should ask your mom."

Placing both hands on her cheeks, I pull her forward until our mouths crash together. "I love you, silly girl." Once I release her, I drop down to my knee and fish the ring I bought for her a month ago out of my pocket, and hold it up. Her mouth drops open and she quickly covers it.

"Kai?"

"Alexandria, I have been in love with you since the moment I laid eyes on you. Will you do me the honor of being my wife, my partner, the one I fall asleep with every night and the one I wake to every morning?"

Alex nods rapidly. "Yes, so many times yes."

I slip the ring on her finger before I drop it in the sand. I hadn't really thought out my proposal, but as soon as she asked me, I had to ask her.

"And yes, I asked your dad ... sort of."

"What do you mean, sort of?"

Kissing her ring, I stand and pull her into my arms.

"Your dad has been hinting for a long time that he'd be way okay if I were his son-in-law. I kept telling him soon."

"That's because he loves you."

I shake my head. "It's because he loves you and he knows that I'll never do anything to hurt you. I love you, Alex."

"I love you, Kai, but ... you didn't exactly answer my question."

I can't help but laugh. "Yes, Alex. I'll marry you. Just name the time and place, and I'll be there ... by the way, I know a really good caterer!"

THE END

DARK ROOM: A Society X Novel

BY HEIDI MCLAUGHLIN & L.P. DOVER

Parker

Never in a million years did I think I'd be pulling into the parking lot of Society X; the whole sex club scene just isn't for me. I have far too much to lose if I'm caught with my pants around my ankles. And if it weren't for my fraternity brother, Bryce Adams, I wouldn't be here. But when a brother calls, you come running . . . even if it's to a place where you could lose your life savings and A-list clientele.

Bryce is offering me an investment deal. One he says will only come along once in a lifetime. In college, he'd had this harebrained scheme none of us thought would take off. The first thing the brilliant jackass did was Trademark his idea. Then, with a ferocity none of us knew he possessed, he not only chased after his dream, he accomplished it. However, considering the nature of the business, banks won't touch him.

That's where I come in.

After my grandfather died, I inherited his company.

227

Ward Enterprises is a Fortune 500 who buys or invests in companies in financial ruin, keeping them afloat until we decide to sell our stock back; or if the market is treating us well, we stay on and take profit.

Society X doesn't exactly meet any of the aforementioned situations, but that doesn't mean Ward Enterprises isn't interested—even dirty money is money.

Before I can knock on the door marked *Employees Only*, it swings open and Bryce greets me with a hug. Stepping back, I take him in: holey jeans, black dress shoes, white button down, and a mop top full of blond locks. Not a single thing has changed about him since college, except for the fact he's now a *rich*, horny motherfucker.

"Man, look at you." I shake my head at his attire and smile.

"Fuck off, bro. You're in a three-piece?"

"That's because I have to meet with fucknuts like you all day."

He barks out a laugh and holds the door open for me to enter. Coming here, I'd expected to walk into a dark hallway permeated with the stench of sex, so I'm pleasantly surprised to find a pristine entryway lined with Andy Warhol paintings.

"I thought you fucked for a living?"

"Nah, not me. But my employees do. Well, some of them do. Some don't. I'm getting ahead of myself. Let me show you." The hallway opens up into a network of passages and we take a series of turns until he's typing in a code and opening a door. When we step through, there's an entryway with blacked out windows, a coatroom, and a pay station. "For you to get the full effect, we need to start at the beginning."

"I'm listening."

"All visitors—both men and women—filter through this door." He points behind me and I nod. "They pay and check all personal items over there. There are absolutely no cell phones, cameras, or any recording devices allowed past this point. Most people who have been here before leave their shit in their cars.

"When they're done here, they have a choice of one of two doors: *Men* or *Women*. They pick their door and enter, waiting for an usher to meet them at the end of the walkway."

Bryce opens the door to women. *Thank God.* I'm not sure I can stomach watching men grind their banana hammocks all over women, at least not after the lunch I had. He waves to the man standing at the end of the short walkway, which is filled with pictures of the dancers and merchandise they have for sale.

"This isn't open seating. The earlier you arrive, the better your seats. We have ushers on each side who will seat you and your party. The last thing I need are crazy bitches starting fights in my club."

There's a partition blocking the view from the walkway, so the only way to see who is in the club or on stage is by being escorted in. I guess it saves them from having peeping toms who are getting off in line.

As soon as I step around the partition, the floor plan opens up. In the center of the room is the stage, complete with a pole and a half-naked chick hanging from it. At the back, there is a row of private, half-circle booths. Most of them seat four people, while some are put together for larger parties. Everything is decorated in white, making it appear pristine.

"What's with the mirrors?" I ask, curious as to why they would line the walls with floor to ceiling mirrors.

"Lap dances are a bit more exciting when you can watch her grind on your cock from all angles. It's a fetish thing."

"I see." I say it, but I don't really mean it, because this is definitely not my scene. I've never had to pay for sex or come looking for carnal entertainment.

"The men's side has an identical set up, but it's the center I need to show you. Actually, it's *because* of the center I can't go to the bank and ask for a loan to expand. Follow me."

He has me intrigued. Following him down the hall, I notice there are both male and female restrooms. The thought hadn't occurred to me that women probably come here too.

Coming to yet another door, Bryce types in a code. From what I'm gathering, everything outside these walls is secured and with limited access, which is a huge selling point.

"The hallways intersect and are designed for employees only." We walk a few feet until we come to three doors marked *1*, *2*, and *3*. "No one is allowed back here without an escort. Doors leading in and out of this area are monitored by camera and locked with a keypad. And only certain staff members are allowed access.

"These rooms are for members who we've tagged as elite. They fill out an application, something they can only do one time. If chosen, they have access to a room with a reservation."

"What are these rooms?"

"Sex rooms – all done consensually and without cost."

"You let people have sex in here for free?" How would he make money if that's the case? The cover charge is only fifteen dollars, with a one drink minimum per table requirement.

"Membership fees. If you're chosen to become a Society X member, you have to pay a monthly fee and are given either a necklace or a bracelet. It's how you know who's eligible for a little extra party. The process to become elite is strict, though. Women get one free fuck and it's up to the partner to provide feedback on her abilities. If she's a dud, her application is tossed aside, but if she lets her inhibitions go and rocks your fucking world, we want to keep her around."

"And what about the women, are they providing feedback on the men?"

"Of course," Bryce says with a shrug. "But if they're getting their big O, most women won't complain. They may, however, request that they not encounter that particular guy again."

"I see." I'm trying to comprehend how all of this is legal and what the ramifications would be if I were to invest and the club gets raided. "You're running a brothel."

Bryce shakes his head adamantly. "The sex is *free*. You're paying a membership fee to the club, which includes private dances, house drinks, and the VIP section. If you choose to take a patron or dancer into a room for some one-on-one time – it's completely legal. I wouldn't ask you to do this if we'd run the risk of getting shut down by the Feds."

I'm still not convinced, but I'm also not one to give up on a business deal until I've had a chance to dot my I's and cross my T's. Each transaction is different and they need to be treated as such. "Let me see the rooms."

Bryce walks to door three and types in the code. Upon entering, I immediately want to leave, but hold my footing. The walls are painted a deep purple, almost black. There's a padded table in the center of the room with chains dangling from the sides. Hanging from the wall are an assortment of whips, chains and other things such as candles, feathers and a saw-horse contraption.

"People come in here a lot?"

"It's one of our most booked rooms because you're allowed to get your freak on without anyone knowing. People know if they break the rules, they're out. There are no second chances at Society X."

"What are the rules?"

"No names or numbers, everything is anonymous. Each member enters a room at their own risk."

I nod, understanding why those rules would be in place. The thought intrigues me – the ability to have anonymous sex without the hassle of getting to know someone. "Are all of the rooms the same set up?"

"Nah, man. We got a little something for everyone. I'll show you." We go to the door marked with the number two. "This is the viewing room. You set your scene and watch it play out. We have a couple who has been married for a few years, but the husband has issues getting it up so he comes in here to watch his wife get fucked."

This room is completely different from the first. The walls are lighter and instead of a table, there's a circular couch facing the back wall. The wall is covered in red velvet curtains framing a stage. And right fucking now, on that stage, are two women sharing a double-headed dildo.

"Should we be in here?" I ask under my breath, unable to take my eyes off the ladies.

He nods to the women who are watching us as they fuck each other. "Of course. They work here, and wanted to give you a little show." He looks at me with a cocked eyebrow and laughs. He knows I'm turned on. I'd have to be dead to not find two women fucking sexier than hell.

"What about hygiene?" The question is a cover. I need to get out of this room before I whip my cock out and find out which woman wants to suck me off. Fuck, I'd take them both and let one sit on my face while the other rides me.

"We have a cleaning service that comes in after each use and disinfects the room. As far as the patrons go, everything is at your own risk, so cover your junk up."

"You know I could never—"

"Yeah, yeah . . . I've had a lot of men say this isn't for them. But it's all about releasing pent up stress. Having sex with a stranger is the most exhilarating experience of your life. Take those girls up there." He pointed to the stage. "I know you want to get in the middle of that shit and find out which one sucks cock better; it's in our nature. Society X lets you embrace it."

"I can see that." The women toss the dildo aside and assume the sixty-nine position, making my cock ache. Bryce slaps me on the shoulder, laughing. He knows I'm sold.

"Come on. If you like this room, you'll fucking love the dark room."

VIEWING ROOM: A Society X Novel

BY HEIDI MCLAUGHLIN & L.P. DOVER

Kennedy

The day finally came, and for the first time in seven years I'm able to breathe. I hate that I feel like this, but when you're strapped down for so long, the feeling of being free is just so liberating.

"I don't think I've ever seen you smile like that," Chris observes, walking into my office. Chris Marshall is my business partner and one of my closest friends. We graduated college together and started up our own law firm. For three years now, *Marshall & Vaughn* has been the most highly sought out law firm in Portland.

Smiling wide, he sits down in front of my desk, his green eyes lit with excitement and his blond hair gelled to perfection; he's ready for our night out. Glancing down at the paper in my hands, I breathe a sigh of relief.

"It's because I've never had a reason to. The only thing that's made me happy over the past few years is this firm."

With a failing marriage, I had to put my focus into

something. Neither Aaron nor I wanted to put forth the effort to keep our relationship intact, so we went our separate ways. We married too young and had different goals in life. There were plenty of good times shared, but it wasn't enough. I can't even begin to tell you how long it's been since we've had sex.

Leaning over on his arms, Chris winks. "All of that's about to change, my dear friend. Now that you're officially divorced we're going out to celebrate. No more late nights at the office for you."

Chris is the one who tried to persuade me not to marry Aaron in the first place, that he wasn't the right kind of guy for me. I wish I would've listened to him, but my parents loved Aaron and I wanted to make them happy. Now I know to do things that make me happy; work is my escape.

"Oh yeah? How are you going to stop me?"

His eyes twinkle and I know I'm in trouble; he's up to something. It's confirmed when Elaine and Sara appear in the doorway, dressed for a night out on the town. Elaine's wearing a short, flared black dress that looks sophisticated with her pixie-style brown hair while Sara looks sexy with her curly blonde hair pulled high to show off her shoulders in her strapless red dress.

"Where are you off to?" I ask them.

They glance at each other and smile. "The same place you are," Sara informs me.

I glance down at my black skirt and blue blouse, knowing I'm not dressed for whatever it is they're planning. Elaine waves me off. "You look amazing, Kennedy. You could wear a plastic bag and still be as beautiful as ever."

"That's right," Sara agrees. "You'll fit right in where we're going."

Sara is our receptionist and in her early thirties just like me. Chris and I became friends with her in law school, but she dropped out to help support her parents who were ill. Now that they're both gone, she's hoping to finish up her schooling. Elaine, on the other hand, is in her forties and happily married with a son in high school. She's mine and Chris' assistant.

Chris holds out his hand. "There's a party in your honor tonight. The girls and I have been planning it all week."

Taking his hand, I walk around the edge of my desk to join them. "A party? Where?"

They all grin at each other and then Chris waggles his brows at me. "Let's just say it's about damn time you went there with me."

Heart racing, I can't believe what I'm hearing. *Is he talking about Society X?* It's an elite club Chris is a member of and I've often been curious about it, but never wanted to go while I was married. Even though Aaron and I were done a long time ago, I felt I should wait until our divorce was final. Now there's nothing holding me back.

"Are you trying to say we're going to Society X?" I ask.

Just being able to go inside is a thrill in itself. Chris told me numerous stories of his times there in the sex rooms. Society X is a club where you can experience an upscale, striptease type atmosphere and if you're a member you can enjoy a lot more. Only high profile people can afford to be a member but Chris said it's worth it.

Chris pulls me toward the door. "Yep, and we've all banded together to make sure you have the best night of your life."

Sara nods happily as we walk past. "It's called the Big D party. The people at the club loved the idea."

"Great," I laugh. *I can't wait.*

When we get out to the parking lot, I climb into my car

and follow them there. The club is packed when we arrive, a line wrapping around the building. We all park and Chris opens my door. "You ready?"

Exiting the car, I point at the line. "How are we going to get in? It'll take hours."

Sara and Elaine join us, both thinking the same thing by the expressions on their faces. Chris chuckles and puts his arm around me. "That's because those people aren't members." We walk up to the front of the club and the guy standing at the door waves us up. He has a handsome face with the brightest blue eyes I've ever seen and muscular arms. The way he looks at Chris leads me to believe they know each other; it has to be Max, his infamous cousin.

Leaning down, Chris whispers in my ear, "That's my cousin."

"I figured," I say with a smile. "I can almost see the family resemblance."

Chris beams. "Really? You think I'm that hot?"

I wink. "Maybe you can get a job here." He stands up straighter and I can't help but laugh. Chris is a very attractive man, always turning women down left and right. Before I met Aaron, my parents fell in love with Chris. They never understood why we didn't date until I told them he was gay. My mother always said it was unfair how all the good looking guys preferred men. I have to agree with her.

Max saunters up to me and shakes my hand. "You must be Kennedy. I've heard a lot about you. I'm Max. I'll be the one showing you around the club."

"It's good to meet you. I've heard a lot about you, too," I say, winking up at Chris.

He flourishes a hand toward the door. "Shall we?"

Sara jumps ahead of us and holds onto Elaine's arm as we walk inside. Max and Chris are behind me, whispering words I can't hear but it's obviously funny by the sound of their chuckles.

There's a stopping point up ahead where people are asked to leave their things. Apparently, no phones are allowed in the club. "Ladies, all you have to do is leave your electronics such as cameras and phones. You're more than welcome to carry your purses in," Max informs us.

We walk up to the front and drop off our things. There are other employees walking around inside and they all look professional, dressed in tuxedos. There's nothing cheap about Society X. From the fixtures to the expensive flooring, you can tell the owner had to spend some serious money to make the club as elite as it is.

Max leads us past the slew of people inside to a hallway that drops us off at two doors. One is labeled *Men* and the other *Women*. Max smiles at us all and opens the door to the Men side. "I'm assuming this is where you want to go, right?"

"Um . . . yeah," Sara laughs. "I don't swing the other way."

Giggling, Elaine nudges me in the side. "So she says."

Sara moves up to the door. "I heard that."

Max focuses on me and I nod. He opens the door and the deep thump of the music vibrates from my feet to all through my body. It's dark, but I can see all the different flashes of light above the tall wall. Women holler out and I can only imagine what they're seeing. When we turn the corner, my eyes go wide.

Chris comes up from behind and whispers in my ear, "Ready to get this party started?"

"Yes," I breathe. Chris says something to Max and then it isn't long before I have a drink in my hands.

There are men everywhere, walking around half-naked

and talking to the women. I've never seen so many gorgeous people in my life. My ex-husband is a decent looking man, but nothing like what I'm seeing. I didn't even know that people like this existed in Portland.

Max leads us over to a private table and we sit. "In about an hour, we have a surprise for you. Actually, it was Chris' idea. He thought it'd be just what you needed."

Eyes wide, I suck in a breath. "You're not going to make me go into the dark room, are you?"

Everyone bursts out laughing and Chris shakes his head. "No, crazy woman. You're not ready for that. But what's going to happen is just as exciting. You'll thank me tomorrow."

Is it wrong that I'm excited? I'm thirty-three years old and it feels like I'm back in college, having fun without a care in the world. I've missed so many good years being stuck with Aaron.

Society X is known for its sex clubs. If you're a member, you can choose between three rooms: the dark room, the viewing room, or the bondage room. The dark room is where you're in complete darkness with another person you don't know. It's the appeal of the room, to have sex with a stranger. The thought seems pretty tempting, but I'm more of a visual type of person. The bondage room is completely out for me. I don't like the whips and chains kind of stuff. The viewing room, however, could be very interesting. In there, you can watch whatever fantasy your heart truly desires. Chris loves that room; it's what got him hooked to the club. Some will say he's addicted.

Max brings me another drink and it's just what I need to loosen up. There's so much going on in the club that I have to experience it all. Standing, I reach for my drink. "I'm going to walk around for a bit before my surprise," I tell everyone. Sara starts to get up and join me, but then one of the strippers comes by and begins to talk to her. She mouths the word 'sorry' at me but I wave her off, laughing.

There are tables all throughout the room with ladies filling almost every seat. The guy on stage is dancing for a group of women who keep shoving money down the front of his G-string. It isn't just one-dollar bills either. The women here have money to burn.

My gaze roams around the room until a certain man catches my attention. He's younger than me, but probably not by much, maybe in his mid-twenties. His body is amazing, but it's his face that got me. There are ladies all around him, but for some reason, he has his eyes on me. They're dark, most likely a shade of brown from what I can tell. I bite my lip and try not to smile, but it's hard not to. It's been so long since I've had a man look at me like that.

"Good evening," a voice calls out from behind. My heart jumps and I turn around, gasping for air. A guy in one of the Society X tuxedos holds a hand out to me. "I'm Jared. You're Kennedy Vaughn, correct?" He has dark hair, gelled in messy spikes, and a really cute smile.

I shake his hand. "Yes," I reply curiously.

He hands me a card. "We've been watching you tonight. If you're interested, I'd love to talk to you more about becoming a member. We think you'll be a good addition to our clientele."

"Is that something you say to all the ladies?" I ask with a laugh.

His gaze turns serious. "No, Ms. Vaughn. We're very particular with the people we choose. I know Mr. Marshall has something planned for you tonight, but if you're willing, I'd love to invite you back for a tour of the rest of the club. That is, if you're interested."

It takes all I have not to look at the mysterious guy across the room, but I can feel his eyes on me. "Thank you, Jared. I'll think about it and let you know."

He nods once and smiles. "Sounds good, Ms. Vaughn. I look forward to hearing back from you."

He saunters off and I turn around, my heart falling when I can't spot my guy. He's probably off in a back room rubbing up on someone else. Why do I care anyway? He's most likely gay just like most of the men who work in strip clubs.

Tossing back the rest of my drink, I take one last look around the room and am about to head over to my table when a voice murmurs in my ear, "Looking for me?"

Gasping, I turn around. It's the guy from across the room and I'm right about his eyes—they're a soft brown with a gold ring around his pupils; very sexy. His cologne wafts in the air and it's intoxicating. It takes all I have not to run my fingers down his rock hard abs.

"You're a little full of yourself, aren't you?" I counter.

He shrugs. "Not really. I was just hoping you were. My name's Hunter." He reaches for my hand and keeps his gaze on mine as he kisses it. My body shivers and a smile crosses his lips. "I haven't seen you in here before."

He slowly lets my hand go and I have to remind myself to breathe. "I'm Kennedy. It's my first time here. Apparently, my colleagues thought it'd be a good idea to celebrate my divorce."

His smile widens. "And the night is getting better. You don't look old enough to have been married. Must not have lasted long."

"Five years. We were just two different people. And I'm not as young as you may think."

His gaze roams over my body in appreciation, making

everything inside of me tighten. "You can't be more than thirty."

"Thirty-three," I correct him. "And you're what ... twenty-one?" I know he's older than that, but it's fun flirting with him. I'm never going to see him again after tonight, so why not?

He bites his lip. "Twenty-five. How old is your ex-husband?"

"Thirty-six, why?"

I can feel the warmth of his body as he moves closer, his lips only a breath away. "Just thought I'd see if you'd be interested in someone younger. I'm positive I could make you feel things your ex-husband couldn't."

My body trembles and thoughts of sneaking away to a dark corner with him run rampant in my mind. However, like all strip clubs, they're made to speak like that. He's probably said the same thing to a dozen other women within the past hour.

I step back. "Thanks for the offer, but aren't most of you gay?" The words are out of my mouth before I can stop them.

He tries to hold back his smile and fails. His fingers grasp a strand of my auburn hair and he twirls it around. "I'm not gay, Kennedy," he murmurs, drawing closer. "If you stick around long enough, maybe you'll find that out."

"Kennedy," Chris calls. I jerk around and he's standing with Sara and Elaine, waving me over. Hunter has already walked off but makes sure to glance at me over his shoulder as we retreat to opposite ends of the room. Chris glances at Hunter and then at me. "I see you're mingling tonight. He's cute."

I smack his arm. "Not going to happen."

"Are you ready for your surprise? Max is ready for us," Sara says excitedly.

I laugh. "I guess so." Max waits for us by another door that leads out of the stripping area. When he opens it, there's a long hallway with other doors.

We follow Max to a door on the left, but he stops with his hand on the knob, his gaze on mine. "You don't have to participate if you don't want to, but Chris thought you'd enjoy it. I wanted to go ahead and warn you now."

My heart thunders in my chest. "What exactly will I be doing?"

He nods toward the room. "This is the viewing room. We have a dancer all picked out for you, but your friends have requested to have you up on stage with him. Basically, all it'll be is a lap dance."

"And we get to watch," Sara pipes in. "But I'll be happy to switch places with you."

Chris puts his arm around me. "Nope, this is something she has to do. It's time she lives a little bit."

As Max opens the door, I take a deep breath. I'm ready.

Acknowledgments

We want to thank you, the readers, for allowing us to bring you Society X. We hope you enjoyed Dark Room, Viewing Room and now Play Room, as much as we've enjoyed writing the series.

Deciding to collaborate is a leap of faith. You have to put your trust into someone else and that's not always easy. With that said, we are not done! We have a few new stories up our sleeves that we think you'll enjoy.

Thank you to our families for not only their support, but guidance and understanding.

And last, but not least...

Letitia Hasser. We can't thank you enough for rebranding our series. We love our new covers!

Thank you! Thank you for taking the time to read our words. Not only with Society X, but our solo projects as well.

Much love,

Heidi & Leslie

About Heidi McLaughlin

Heidi is a New York Times and USA Today Bestselling author.

Originally from the Pacific Northwest, she now lives in picturesque Vermont, with her husband and two daughters. Also renting space in their home is an over-hyper Beagle/Jack Russell, Buttercup and a Highland West/Mini Schnauzer, JiLL and her brother, Racicot.

When she's isn't writing one of the many stories planned for release, you'll find her sitting court-side during either daughter's basketball games.

Forever My Girl, is set to release in theaters on January 26, 2018, starring Alex Roe and Jessica Rothe.

Connect with Heidi

www.heidimclaughlin.com
heidi@heidimclaughlin.com

About L.P. Dover

New York Times and USA Today Bestselling author, L.P. Dover, is a southern belle residing in North Carolina along with her husband and two beautiful girls. Before she even began her literary journey she worked in Periodontics enjoying the wonderment of dental surgeries.

Not only does she love to write, but she loves to play tennis, go on mountain hikes, white water rafting, and you can't forget the passion for singing. Her two number one fans expect a concert each and every night before bedtime and those songs usually consist of Christmas carols.

Aside from being a wife and mother, L.P. Dover has written countless novels including her Forever Fae series, the Second Chances series, the Gloves Off series, the Armed & Dangerous series, the Royal Shifters series, and her standalone novel, Love, Lies, and Deception. Her favorite genre to read is romantic suspense and she also loves writing it. However, if she had to choose a setting to live in it would have to be with her faeries in the Land of the Fae.

Connect with L.P.

www.lpdover.com
authorlpdover@gmail.com

Also by Heidi McLaughlin

THE BEAUMONT SERIES

Forever My Girl – Beaumont Series #1

My Everything – Beaumont Series #1.5

My Unexpected Forever – Beaumont Series #2

Finding My Forever – Beaumont Series #3

Finding My Way – Beaumont Series #4

12 Days of Forever – Beaumont Series #4.5

My Kind of Forever – Beaumont Series #5

The Beaumont Boxed Set - #1

THE ARCHER BROTHERS

Here with Me

Choose Me

Save Me

Lost in You Series

Lost in You

Lost in Us

THE BOYS OF SUMMER

Third Base

STANDALONE TITLE

.

84401027R00156

Made in the USA
Middletown, DE
19 August 2018